like you CARE

DEVILBEND DYNASTY: BOOK ONE

INTERNATIONAL BESTSELLING AUTHOR

KAYDENCE SNOW

Cover Design by Sara Eirew
Editing by Kirstin Andrews
Formatting by AB Formatting
kaydencesnow.com

For CoraLee June
This book wouldn't exist if it wasn't for you

PROLOGUE

THE CABLE TIE AROUND MY WRISTS WAS SO tight my fingers were going numb. The pole they'd tied me to dug into my back, the cold metal and the evening breeze making me shiver.

Or maybe I was shivering from fear.

They'd never gone this far before, never hurt me this badly.

I sobbed, the flood of tears stinging my sore cheek.

The knife was small—just a little switchblade thing—but it looked sharp. A shudder raced down my spine as the tip was dragged gently down my throat, the middle of my chest, my belly.

For the first time, I wondered if I would actually survive this night. Were they really about to kill me? Did their hatred really run that deep?

Movement in the distance caught my attention. Someone was sprinting toward us across the football field.

My heart soared . . . then I recognized him, and it

plummeted again.

He stopped just a few feet away, breathing hard, his wide eyes taking in the whole fucked-up scene. He couldn't hide his reaction; his beautiful face gave it all away—surprise, horror, disbelief, disgust . . . was that anger I saw next?

I couldn't be sure of anything anymore. My soul was being torn to shreds, and my mind was going with it. I had no idea what he'd do next.

Would he join in and help them destroy me?

Would he stand by and do nothing, let it happen?

Would he walk away, like a coward, so he wouldn't have to watch?

Or would he defend me? Save me?

Knowing what I'd just learned, what it would mean, what it would cost, did I even want him to?

He took a step forward, and I braced myself to find out if the boy I loved would be my salvation . . . or if my heart would be torn to shreds right along with my mind and soul.

CHAPTER 1

THE TENNIS BALL THUNKED RHYTHMICALLY AS my cousins got into a lengthy rally. It wasn't even midday yet, but the sun was already unbearable, reflecting brightly off the blue of the tennis court.

Donna and Harlow were in pristine tennis whites right down to their shoes, their skirts swishing around their tanned thighs as they lunged for balls as though competing at a world-class tournament. I was in shorts and a tank top, my flip-flops abandoned under the chair—nothing pristine about any of it. I didn't know the first thing about holding a tennis racket, let alone hitting the ball.

My cousins lived on a property big enough to hold a tennis court *and* a pool. I lived in an apartment off a hallway that always smelled like curry. This was not my world, but these girls were the closest thing I had to friends.

The rally broke, and Donna grunted a "yes" as she pumped her fist.

"Are you two nearly done?" Amaya yelled from the chair next to me before taking a sip of her watermelon juice. She went to Fulton Academy with my cousins and lived on the next street. They'd been friends since preschool, so she was always around when I was around. Not that I minded. I liked her confidence—if only some of it would rub off on me . . .

"Yeah, some of us would like to get in the pool," I added.

"We need to finish this," Harlow ground out before crouching down, waiting for her sister to serve.

Amaya and I both groaned and slumped down in our chairs. We were in the shade of a massive umbrella, but it felt as if the sun was beating right through it onto the top of my head. I drank the rest of my own watermelon juice, loudly slurping up the last dregs of the sweet liquid through my straw.

Amaya finished hers too, dropped the empty glass on the table between us, and reached for her phone. She changed the song, the new beat thumping out of the little portable speaker, then stretched her arms up over her head. Her perfectly straight, almost black hair hung down the back of the chair, shining like silk. Her long brown legs were toned and perfect.

I wished I had her beautiful skin. I wished I had anyone's skin but my own, especially the skin on my face.

"How was your summer, Mena?" Amaya asked, giving me a genuine, friendly smile. It was the question I'd been dreading all morning.

The three of them had spent most of the summer at some camp with their other rich friends. I'd spent the summer on the cramped little balcony of my apartment, doing elaborate makeup looks and then wiping them off again—when I wasn't working at the diner.

"Pretty chill." I shrugged and hoped she'd drop it.

"Did you do anything fun with your friends?"

Your friends. Not *your other friends* or *your friends from school.* Did she not consider me a friend?

I pushed the choking feeling down and worked hard to keep my expression neutral. "Nothing worth mentioning." *Please drop it.* "I can't stand this heat anymore." I groaned. "I don't know how those two aren't melting."

My cousins were still whacking the tennis ball, sprinting up and down the court.

"Ugh, I know. They're gonna get heatstroke." Amaya took a cigarette out of her pack and lit it.

Seizing the opportunity to avoid the topic of my nonexistent friends, I slipped into my flip-flops. "I'm gonna go get another drink and jump in the pool."

Amaya waved me away with the cigarette held between her elegant fingers. "Hey, you maniacs!" she yelled as I walked up the path toward the house. "We've had enough. You have until I finish this smoke, and then we're getting in that motherfucking pool, or so help me . . ."

My cousins started shouting back, but I could no longer discern what they were saying. I smiled to myself as my shoulders relaxed. I loved hanging out with these

9

girls, but I really didn't want to talk about my life. It was easier to just pretend.

I walked through the Meads' massive house, my flip-flops slapping on marble tile as the AC cooled my flushed skin. My aunt Emily was sitting at the island in the kitchen, flipping through an interior design magazine and sipping on a coffee made for her on the professional espresso machine in their butler's pantry.

She looked up at me and smiled. Donna and Harlow got their blonde hair and athletic bodies from her and their round eyes from their dad.

"You girls having fun?" She brushed my hair off my shoulder as I leaned on the counter next to her.

"Yes." My returning smile was genuine. My mother's sister had never made me feel invisible. She'd also never made me feel awkward about my face or treated me differently because we didn't have the kind of money she had.

"Where are the others?" She glanced behind me, in the direction of the tennis court.

"We're all gonna jump in the pool soon. I just came in to get more watermelon juice." I rolled my eyes and chuckled. " After your daughters are done battling it out for the top spot in the Australian Open."

"In this heat?" She shook her head. "Do I need to go tell them to knock it off?"

"No, no," I rushed out. I didn't want her to catch Amaya smoking. "They're wrapping it up."

My aunt nodded and smoothed my hair again. "OK.

Oh, by the way ..." She hopped off the stool, her understated perfume wafting toward me as she breezed past in a tailored shirt and khaki shorts, not a hair out of place. She picked up a MacBook and coiled-up charger off the side table. "We got Donna and Harlow new laptops for school, so I wanted to give you this one. It's been reset and all that jazz."

"Oh." I took it reflexively, the sleek metal cool in my fingers. "Thank you ..." I trailed off. I really was thankful, but I knew Mom didn't like me taking things from my cousins. My dad would be fine with it. He knew my aunt's gifts came from a good place, and he wasn't too proud to accept the help. But my mom . . .

My aunt saw the uncertainty on my face. "Don't worry about your mom. I'll talk to her. You need a good computer for school."

Her tone brooked no arguments, so I nodded. My current laptop was clunky and constantly crashing—often midsentence as I worked on an assignment. We couldn't possibly afford a new one, so I hadn't even mentioned it to my parents.

Aunt Emily took the laptop out of my hands again and set it on the bench. "You go on out to the pool. I'll have the drinks and a snack brought out to you before I head off to lunch."

"Thanks, Auntie Em."

I did as she said, making my way through the open-plan living area, out through the French doors, and down another manicured path toward the pool. I would much rather have just gone to the fridge and gotten the damn drinks myself than deal with the awkwardness of having a servant bring things, but there was no point arguing with my aunt.

The pool was as ostentatious as the house, with curving edges, natural stone paving, and lush landscaping, complete with stunning views of California's natural landscape. Umbrella-shaded loungers lined one side, towels already placed neatly on each one. I toed off my flip-flops and whipped my tank top off over my head as voices preceded the arrival of the others.

The girls walked up before I could get my shorts off. Donna and Harlow spotted me, and matching evil grins pulled at their faces.

"No," I said as firmly as I could, throwing my arms out in front of me.

They shared a look and sprinted directly for me. Neither one seemed to give a shit that they were still fully clothed in their tennis gear as they tackled me into the water. All three of us splashed into the pool in a tangle of limbs and hair.

"Oh man, that's refreshing," Harlow yelled as we surfaced, spluttering and laughing. They waded to the edge of the pool and got out, removing their sodden tennis shoes.

"You guys are such dicks!" I smacked the water on either side of me, but I couldn't help the smile tugging at my face.

"Hey, you wanted to get in the pool," Donna teased, and I flipped her off. Somehow, her short, sleek haircut still looked neat and cute even plastered to her head.

"You *did* want to get in the pool." Perfectly dry and unruffled, Amaya flipped her shiny black hair over her shoulder, lit another cigarette, and unhurriedly lowered her perfect ass to one of the loungers.

The sisters headed to the pool house to get their bathing suits, shedding wet white clothing as they went.

"Whose side are you on?" I arched a brow at Amaya as I headed toward the ladder, the denim tight around my hips. The shorts would be a pain in the ass to get off.

"Mine." She shrugged. "Always mine."

Just as I reached the ladder, a servant in black shorts and a collared T-shirt came down the path, carrying a tray laden with drinks and snacks.

I ducked my head and pushed off the ladder, diving back under the water. Better to deal with the wet denim for a few more minutes than deal with someone I didn't know looking at my gross face.

I surfaced at the deep end and took big gulps of air, facing the verdant plants on the other side of the pool.

"He's gone," Amaya announced. She had stripped down to a white bikini that practically glowed against her smooth dark skin, her black hair gathered into a messy bun on top of her head.

I sighed in relief and swam back to the ladder. She gave me a warm smile as she waded in at the shallow end. The girls knew how self-conscious I was of my face, but they also knew I didn't like talking about it.

Donna and Harlow came back out wearing

swimsuits that probably cost more than my whole wardrobe, with geometric mesh cutouts, and joined us in the pool.

"I wish you went to our school, Mena." Harlow pouted.

"Yeah, senior year would be epic with all of us together," Donna agreed. Donna was born eleven months before Harlow, making them as close in age as sisters could be without being twins.

I nodded before kicking my legs up to float on my back. "Me too."

I'd have given anything to go to their fancy private school, where I'd actually have friends. But I was stuck at my shitty public school, where I wished I didn't exist— on a good day.

We spent the rest of the day by the pool, listening to music and talking, the girls telling me about their time away. We had lunch brought to us and hardly left the loungers other than to cool off in the water.

We all took photos on our phones, but when Amaya went to post one with all four of us squished into the frame, drinking watermelon juice through straws, I made her promise not to. I didn't want anyone seeing the repulsive thing on my face, and I really didn't want anything online that could be used against me. They argued with me, but I was pretty stubborn on this front, so Amaya ended up posting one with just the three of them. As usual, she added #DevilbendDynasty to the caption.

They'd started using the phrase last year, after we

found a stack of photo albums in the Meads' attic—our moms and grandmothers, generations of Devilbend women, in social clubs, at charity functions, sticking together, supporting one another. I knew the girls wanted to include me in the sentiment, but I wasn't dynasty material—I was just a poor, ugly girl with no future.

My mom picked me up on her way home from work, coming inside to catch up with her sister while I squeezed in every last moment with the girls. I was pretty sure they argued about the laptop, but it came home with us, so my aunt must have won.

The carefree, light feeling I'd had hanging out with the girls was pushed out of my chest with every mile that took me farther away from them. As the manicured lawns and immaculate, tall fences gave way to tightly packed concrete buildings on the fifteen-minute drive home, some of that concrete settled on my shoulders, my reality weighing me down.

"Did you have fun with your cousins?" Mom asked as we parked in the lot behind our building. It was the first thing she'd said since we got in the car, both of us lost in our thoughts.

I sighed. "Yeah."

"Well, don't sound so enthusiastic about it." She chuckled.

I didn't answer, and she was too tired to prod me any further. My mom had the same blonde hair as my aunt Em, but I got my thick, light brown hair from my dad. I also got his pale blue eyes. If only I had some of his height too. He towered over both my mom and me—but then, most people did.

After dinner and a shower, I went out to the balcony to let my hair air-dry.

The sun was beginning to set, casting everything in a warm yellow-orange hue. Even the shitty side of Devilbend—with the squat apartment buildings, the run-down park, and the shady area near the train station—looked kind of pretty in this light.

But it was an illusion. Under the golden light and summer shadows was hard concrete and graffiti, people struggling to survive, and *me*. I'd had an amazing day, but it made the evening even more bitter by comparison. *Back to reality*. Tomorrow I'd have to go to work at the diner—I'd picked up as many shifts as I could during summer. Then on Monday, it was back to school.

I rubbed the side of my nose and sighed, wishing for the millionth time I could scrub the ugly mark off. Wishing I could change just one thing about my life.

That was impossible, so I decided to paint the pretty sunset onto my face in the form of a smoky but vibrant eye makeup.

"Motherfucker!" My chair scraped against the balcony floor as I leapt up to avoid getting splatters of foundation on my white shorts. The bottle had just slipped out of my hand and smashed on the table. "Fucking *fuck*. God *damn* it!"

I growled in frustration as more than fifty dollars' worth of goop, perfectly matched to my skin tone, went oozing over the edge.

"You all right over there?" A deep male voice came from the balcony next to ours, a shadow shifting behind the bamboo screen my mother had put up for privacy.

"Shit." I froze, heat spreading up my cheeks. That was all I needed—some asshole to tell me off over my potty mouth.

CHAPTER 2

"YES. I'M FINE. JUST DROPPED SOMETHING. sorry about the cursing," I scrambled to reply, hoping he wouldn't demand to speak with my parents.

He chuckled, sounding more amused now than concerned. "I don't give a flying fuck about the cursing." His voice was smooth—like the ocean on a calm day. Mellow and even on the surface, but underneath . . .

I smiled and relaxed my shoulders. "Well . . . fucking great then." I rolled my eyes at myself.

"Must've been something important."

"What?" I frowned, inching closer to the bamboo screen.

"The thing you dropped?"

"Oh!" I'd almost forgotten about the foundation. "Yeah, it was . . . expensive and . . . er . . . never mind."

I suddenly felt shy. I didn't want this random stranger with the beautiful voice to know I'd been that upset over makeup. I didn't want him to think I was conceited.

"Fine. Keep your secrets."

I could hear the smile in his voice. It made me smile too, but I ironed out my expression so he wouldn't hear it. "Why would I trust you with my secrets? You're a stranger. You could be an axe murderer."

His laughter trickled through the tiny gaps in the bamboo and wrapped itself around my shoulders, sending a little shiver down my spine.

"I'm not a stranger. I'm your neighbor. You can trust me," he said.

I realized I was just standing motionless in the middle of my balcony, staring at the bamboo partition. I reached for the roll of paper towels on the table and started cleaning up the mess. "Never trust someone who says *trust me*," I quipped.

"Touché." He chuckled again. "I'll just have to earn your trust the old-fashioned way."

"A cavity search?" I paused mid-wipe. Had I really just said that to a random?

But he didn't even pause before answering. "I was gonna say drug screening, and you jump straight to finger in the ass? Brutal!"

"I don't fuck around." A laugh escaped at the end, part of it slight hysteria from the rush of relief that he hadn't taken offence.

"No, you do not, neighbor."

I couldn't get enough of his smooth voice; his relaxed, casual tone was putting me at ease in a way I never had been with a person I'd never met. Was it the screen between us that allowed me to talk to him without feeling self-conscious about my face? Or was it *him*?

I couldn't tell how old he was just from his voice. Not elderly, that much was clear, but was he my age? A college guy? Maybe he was in his thirties and married with three kids. I really hoped I wasn't flirting with an old dude.

Was that what I was doing? Flirting?

I cleared my throat and deposited the last of the dirty paper towels into a handbasket, then wiped my hands with micellar water to get the foundation off. "So, you just moved in?"

The apartment had been empty for months. Their balcony was right next to ours, but that didn't make us neighbors exactly. Our apartment was the last one at the end of the hallway on the eighth floor. Theirs was the last one at the end of their hallway, but we had to use separate entrances to the building. There were five entrances total—twelve floors of cramped apartments, thousands of people literally living on top of one another.

"Yeah, yesterday. Although I'm questioning the decision."

"New neighbor scaring you off? Am I the one giving off axe murderer vibes now?"

"Hah! Nah. It's the smell."

I frowned and silently sniffed at my underarms. I'd just showered. I smelled like strawberries. "The smell?"

"Yeah. The whole apartment smells like feet."

"Ugh, gross!"

"You have no idea! Every single room. Even the kitchen! If it hadn't rained last night, I would've slept out here."

I laughed. "Have you tried, uh, cleaning it?"

"Yes, thank you, smart-ass. We only got the keys yesterday. My dad had to work all day, so I did what I could on my own. Shampooing the carpets seems to have helped."

He hadn't mentioned a wife and kids! I did a little fist pump. He lived with his dad, but that didn't mean he was my age. Oh god! What if he was, like, twelve, and he was just one of those kids whose voice had dropped early?

"Well," I said, "I hope you get the feet smell out. It's a shame we didn't meet sooner. I could've told you this was a shitty place to live."

"We've had worse. Trust me. Plus, if we hadn't moved in here, I never would've gotten to talk to you."

I bit my bottom lip to hold in the grin and leaned back in the chair. I had no idea what to say to that.

The sun had set; with my window of natural light for makeup application gone, I started to pack everything into my case. After the zip made an obnoxiously loud sound, he cleared his throat and spoke again.

"I'm sorry. Was that ... weird?" Gone was the casual confidence.

"No!" I rushed out, then took a breath to calm my tone. "Not at all. Sorry. I just ... got distracted. I like talking to you too." I cringed.

"Good." I could hear the smile in his voice again.

"So, you move around a lot?" I blurted to fill the silence.

"Yeah. We . . . my dad's . . . yes, we move around a lot."

Maybe he was as nervous and flustered as me. Why did that make my chest feel all warm and fuzzy?

The kitchen light flicked on inside. Mom or Dad would be checking on me any minute now. I didn't want them to know I was talking to . . . whoever this was.

"Shit. I gotta go."

"Oh, OK. Nice talking to you!"

"You too!"

I ducked inside and closed the sliding door behind me just in time.

"I was just about to come check on you, Sweet Chilly." Dad leaned on the kitchen counter and chugged a glass of water. My full name was Philomena Ann Willis. At some point, before I had a say in it, my parents had started calling me Sweet Chilly Philly, and it stuck. The girls called me Mena. The assholes at school called me . . . *Ugh!* I pushed the thought out of my head. I still had a few days before I had to deal with *them*.

I smiled and poured myself a glass too. Mom was snoring lightly on the couch.

"I'm going to bed," I said.

"This early?" We both glanced at the time on the microwave: 9:38 p.m.

"I've got work tomorrow." It wasn't a lie. One of the waitresses had called in sick, and I was more than happy to take the double shift. It would help me replace the foundation I'd just lost.

"Early one?"

"Yeah. Can I get a lift?" I'd get there half an hour early if Dad dropped me off before heading to work, but it would be better than walking and taking the bus in this heat.

"Sure thing."

"Good night."

"Night." He waved me off, heading to wake up Mom.

The next day, I got home from my double shift around ten. Mom was already drifting off on the couch, but she startled awake when I came in and offered to heat up the casserole they'd had for dinner.

"No thanks. I ate at the diner." The pay was shitty, but at least Leah—the owner of the aptly named Leah's Diner—fed us when we worked long shifts. Leah had been friends with my mom in high school, and they'd reconnected when we'd moved back to Devilbend just before I started high school. Just before my life turned into hell on earth.

Actually, high school wasn't hell—it was more like limbo. It wasn't constant daily torture, although there was some of that too. No, it was punishment through alienation. Unless I was being sneered at, laughed at, or having something thrown at me, I didn't exist.

Most of the time I preferred it that way— preferred that people didn't look at me. Didn't look at the hideous birthmark on my face. But fuck, it was lonely sometimes.

The purple birthmark started at the inner corner of my right eye, pooling out down the side of my nose and the top of my cheek like spilled wine—which was probably why they were called "port-wine stains."

It wasn't raised or bumpy; it wasn't a rash or an infectious disease. It was just something I was born with. Something I couldn't escape. Something I *hated*. Most people stared. Some clearly thought it was contagious, shrinking away from me. The kids at school just used it as fuel for their ridicule.

I took a quick shower, then brought my lotion out to the balcony. As soon as the sliding door was closed and I'd settled myself on the little chair, I heard movement on the other side of the bamboo.

"Neighbor?" There was that ocean voice, immediately making me smile.

"Hey, stranger," I called back, propping one foot on the railing so I could rub lotion into my leg.

"I was just about to head to bed. Glad I caught you. Long day?"

"Yeah. I pulled a double shift." I didn't say where I worked—there was still a chance he was an axe murderer.

"That's rough." He sounded unsure; some of the ease of our banter from the previous night was gone.

"It's OK." I fought to keep my tone casual. "I only work part time, so I'm happy to take the extra shifts when I can." I moved on to my other leg.

He sighed. "I gotta get a job."

"Yeah? What do you do?" This was the part where

he told me he was a professional whatever and way too old for me.

He laughed. "Whatever I can. Although it would be nothing if it were up to my dad."

"Really?" Hope blossomed. Most adults didn't let their parents dictate what they did for work, right?

"Yeah. He'd prefer I focus on . . . other things."

I frowned. Neither of us spoke. That was vague and weird.

"It's getting late. I better go." As he moved, his balcony light threw his shadow over the bamboo screen. He was tall, broad shouldered.

When I didn't speak, he did. "Cute toes."

And then he was gone. The sound of his sliding door closing made me shake my head at my idiocy. Why hadn't I told him good night or something? But hey, I sure was glad I'd let my mom paint my toes that deep red on the weekend. They did look cute.

The next day, I got home just after lunch. Mom and Dad were both at work, and there was nothing to stop me from racing through the apartment like a maniac, changing out of my work uniform and into a T-shirt dress, and launching myself onto the balcony. He wasn't there. I waited all afternoon, going inside only for snacks. The sun was setting and I was packing up after my second makeup look when the slide of a balcony door made me pause.

Someone settled in on the other side of the bamboo screen. My heart leapt into my throat, and my hand froze over my makeup bag, several brushes clutched in my fist.

Then I rolled my eyes at myself and let the brushes drop with a clatter.

"Hey, stranger." This time, I let the smile show in my voice.

"Oh, hey!" He sounded a little surprised. "You're early tonight."

"Didn't work this afternoon. Been sitting out here for hours." *Shit!* I cringed. Now I sounded like a creepy moron who'd been waiting for him all day.

But he didn't skip a beat. "I would've come out sooner, but the smell of feet has finally vacated the premises, and I got dragged into a particularly frustrating campaign on Halo."

"Well, I'm glad to know the stink is gone, but, er, what's a Halo?"

"Oh!" His laugh this time was a little nervous. "It's a video game. But not, like, a kid's game or whatever. It's got a parental advisory and everything. It's super violent, actually. Not that I like it for the violence! It actually requires strong problem-solving skills and . . . I'm rambling."

"Yeah, a bit." I laughed.

"Sorry. I just didn't want you to think I was a kid or anything."

Fuck. How old was he? I was so damn confused.

"I still watch SpongeBob SquarePants on Saturday mornings," I blurted, "if I'm not working. There's just something comforting about cartoons and cereal, ya know?"

"Yeah. Takes me back to a time when everything felt right with the world and I didn't have so much to worry about."

"Yeah . . ." I was a little surprised he understood so immediately. What heavy shit was he dealing with? Was it as bad as the reason I was dreading going back to school? Was it worse?

The following day I had the late shift and was kicking myself for not telling the boy next door I wouldn't be home in the evening. Then I was rolling my eyes for assuming he cared enough to notice I wouldn't be around.

Work was busy—the Saturday night dinner crowd keeping us on our toes, especially considering it was the last weekend before school started. I didn't get home until almost eleven. The apartment was dark and quiet, and my dad went straight to bed after picking me up.

I didn't even bother changing—I just went straight out to the balcony.

"Neighbor?" His voice came as soon as I closed the door. It was softer than usual.

"Hey." I smiled, matching his quiet tone. I guessed we were both aware of the thousands of sleeping people in close proximity. "You're still up."

"Yeah . . ." He didn't sound as happy as he usually did. Maybe it wasn't the late hour keeping his voice muted. "I've been sitting out here for hours. I'm kind of avoiding my dad—he's in a mood. I wanted to hear your voice."

27

That warm feeling in my chest intensified even as my brows drew together. His ocean-deep voice had dropped even further, hinting at tumultuous currents underneath.

I pushed aside the chair I usually sat in and lowered myself to the ground, leaning back against the wall. This was where he usually sat—they'd only just moved in, and I had a feeling there was no patio furniture on their balcony.

We were practically shoulder to shoulder, only the flimsy bamboo between us.

"Are you OK?" I asked.

Silence.

I pressed my hand against the bamboo.

After another beat of silence, I felt pressure against my palm, then, slowly, heat spread through the thin screen. He was pressing his hand against mine.

"What's your name?" he asked, his voice almost a whisper.

He'd ignored my question, but that was OK. Some questions were too hard to answer.

I chewed on my lip but didn't want to keep him waiting too long. Even though I hardly knew him, the urge not to disappoint this boy was strong.

"Mena," I said. I wasn't sure why I didn't tell him my full name. It wasn't that I didn't like it, but I was more myself with him than I'd ever been with a new person. The only people I could remotely consider friends called me Mena, and they were the only ones I could truly be myself with. I wanted to be myself with him.

"Mena," he repeated.

"What's yours?"

He didn't hesitate for a second. "Turner."

I opened my mouth to tell him we weren't strangers anymore, but the sound of his sliding door cut me off.

His hand disappeared, and I curled mine into a loose fist, as if trying to hold on to the warmth.

"Turner?" an older, gruffer voice said. "Who are you talking to?"

"No one." He shuffled away.

I tried not to feel hurt.

"I heard something," the older man—probably his dad—said.

"Maybe it was the neighbors."

The door opened, then closed, and he was gone.

I wrapped my arms around my legs and leaned my head back against the wall. Goose bumps rose on my arms in the chilly night air, but I couldn't seem to make myself move.

CHAPTER 3

MY FEET SPED UP, TRYING TO MATCH THE hammering rhythm of my heart. I had to take a deep breath and force myself to slow down. It was only a fifteen-minute walk to school, but at the rate I was going, I'd make it there in five. I wanted to spend *less* time there, not more. But my legs hadn't gotten the memo and kept trying to break into a sprint.

I didn't want to feel like this.

I growled and made myself stop, closed my eyes tight, and forced a long breath in through my nose and out through my mouth, gripping the straps of my backpack until my knuckles were as white as the stars swimming in my vision. After a few moments, I steeled my resolve and moved forward at a steady pace, trying to distract myself by counting the steps in my head.

The tail end of summer meant another perfectly sunny California morning, but I wished it was cloudy and cold so I could have an excuse to hide inside a hoodie all day. I hoped I would go unnoticed regardless, that it would be the silent treatment. Being ignored was much better than how the first day of junior year had gone down.

I tried to push the memory away, but it forced its way into my mind, as insistent as the hot sun on the back of my head.

First day of school had been hot last year as well. I'd fought to slow my steps then too, but there had been a hint of excitement, a tiny sliver of hope, driving the nervous energy that day.

I'd spent all summer—every moment I wasn't working or hanging out with the girls—learning how to do makeup. I'd watched countless hours of YouTube videos and spent half my pay on new products, brushes, pallets, and all kinds of things I hoped would make me more normal in the eyes of my peers. By the end of the summer, I'd gotten pretty good at it, even practicing on Donna, Harlow, and Amaya.

That day, I'd applied an understated look. My birthmark was covered, my lashes accentuated, my lips natural. I thought I looked pretty good.

I was a fool.

I should've known—in high school, the only thing worse than being different is making an active effort to change the thing that makes you different.

I'd walked into school with my head up, smiled, made eye contact; I even gave Jessica Miller a little wave as I stopped at my locker. Most people shot me surprised looks, not really knowing what to make of the new me. A few even reflexively smiled back.

By lunch, word had spread. No one had said anything to me, of course, but they'd all been talking behind my back. Oblivious, I went into the girls' bathroom off the science wing corridor.

I came out of the stall to find four girls leaning against walls and sinks, watching me with amused smiles. Madison and her friends.

I froze, like a gazelle that had just wandered into a circle of leopards.

"Been holding that all morning?" Steph chuckled, tilting her head. "Sounded like an elephant pissing in there."

"Or a man," Bonnie added, crossing her arms and leaning against the tiles next to the mirror. "Do you pee standing up like a man?"

"Her name *is* Phil." Steph giggled. It would've been a cute sound if they all weren't looking at me with promise in their gazes.

No, no, no, please no. It wasn't supposed to be like this. This year was supposed to be different.

I dropped my gaze to the stained beige tiles and walked to the sink, drawing my shoulders forward to make myself as small as possible. All I could do now was be quiet and hope I could get out of there fast.

"That's it, isn't it?" Steph giggled again. "We've been calling you Phil this whole time, but you really *are* a man, aren't you?"

"Those tits must've cost a fucking fortune, then." Kelsey spoke for the first time, her tone bored, her eyes on her phone. I was dying on the inside, and she was double tapping pics on Insta. *Bitch.* Her comment probably came from jealousy. She was super-model thin but flat chested, and I was comfortably filling out a D cup. Not that I'd ever say that to her out loud. It was easier to silently wait it out. They'd get bored eventually.

"Oh my god." Bonnie giggled, and the others all laughed with her. "Did you—"

"No," Madison cut her off. The laughter died. No one dared interrupt Madison. "She's not a man."

I shut the water off. Steph was blocking my access to the hand drier. I decided to just leave with my hands wet.

Each girl took a step closer to me, as if they'd practiced it, as if they instinctively knew I was about to bolt.

I froze again, tried to calm my breathing so my boobs would stop heaving. I didn't want any more attention on them.

Madison kept speaking. "Can't you see Philomena's turned into a woman? Look how beautifully she's done her makeup."

Her voice was so steady, earnest even, that my eyes snapped up in surprise. She gave me a warm smile, her own makeup impeccable. Her linen shorts and V-neck hung on her perfect frame as though they'd been made for her. She tilted her head slightly and took a strand of my hair, gently twirling it between her fingers. I'd gotten up half an hour early to put a slight wave in my usually dead-straight hair.

I cleared my throat. This had never happened

before. I had no idea what to do. My instincts were screaming to get the fuck away from these monsters, but Madison was saying nice things with a perfectly straight face.

"Your hair is so soft," she whispered, twirling more of it around her manicured finger.

After an extended silence, I cleared my throat again and managed to croak, "Thanks?" It came out sounding like a question.

Madison gathered more of my hair into her hand, tangling her fingers in it, and a heavy dread settled in the pit of my stomach. Her fingers scraped my scalp, and she yanked, making me wince.

The others shifted—predators scenting blood.

Madison laughed. It started out as a light chuckle and quickly turned manic, her wild eyes inches from mine as she laughed literally in my face.

"Thanks?" she mimicked. "Fucking pathetic." She punctuated her words with another yank. I cried out and instinctively reached up to wrap my hands around her wrist.

The others moved, pulling my hands behind my back.

Tears stung my eyes.

"You're not a man, Phil." Madison shook her head, her eyes narrowed. "But you're not a woman either. You're fucking *nothing*. And we can't have you walking around, *lying*, pretending to be *something*. You think covering up that hideous thing on your face makes you better? You're a fucking joke. And we can't have anyone forgetting that, can we?"

No one said anything. My labored breathing echoed off the old, chipped tiles. The side of my head where Madison was still pulling on my hair stung like a bitch, and my neck was starting to hurt from the odd angle. A tear slid down my cheek.

"Can we?!" Madison shouted into my face.

"No." I closed my eyes—the next best thing when I couldn't move my head to lower them.

"Good." She released my hair and patted my head as if I were a dog.

My eyes flew open as the bitches holding me pushed me against the sinks.

Madison walked to the back of the bathroom slowly, calmly. She gripped the handle of a mop that had been left in a bucket in the corner and turned back to face us. What idiot of a janitor had left that out? Bonnie giggled again, as if someone had handed her a puppy. Kelsey took a break from her scrolling to snap a picture as Madison raised the mop out of the bucket.

It splatted on the tiles. She dragged the sodden thing across the bathroom.

"No. Please." I started to struggle, but I had no chance. There were four of them, two of them holding me down. The edge of the sink dug into my lower back as my shoulders pushed against the mirror. "I'll take it off. Just let me go, and I'll take it off right now. Please, Madison, *please*, don't do this."

She stopped in front of me and flipped the mop so the shaggy, dripping head was level with my face. The abrasive smell of bleach hit the back of my throat.

I sobbed, pleading with them to stop, to let me go, but it was pointless.

They held me down as Madison shoved the mop into my face. I coughed and spluttered, the bleach making it hard to breathe, making my eyes water and sting. She roughly wiped at my face with the scratchy, disgusting strings until she was satisfied the makeup had been removed.

The mop clattered to the ground moments before they released me, and I collapsed next to it, sobbing, pushing away from them. But I had nowhere to go; the sinks were already at my back.

On their way out, someone dumped the rest of the filthy gray water over my head.

I gasped and spluttered again, the smell making me gag.

The door closed behind them, and I was alone once again.

I refused to look at myself in the mirror when I finally gathered the strength to pick myself up off the floor. I just wrung out my ruined hair and washed up with clean water, splashing it onto my face over and over.

As I turned the tap off, the door opened again. I flinched and turned to face it, chastising myself for stupidly not getting the fuck out of there before they came back.

But it wasn't them. Jessica Miller stopped in her tracks, her eyes widening as they took in my appearance, the mop and bucket, the water all over the ground.

She'd smiled back that morning, but now the status quo had been reestablished. She lowered her head, turned around, and walked back out of the bathroom without saying anything.

In some ways, that hurt even more than what those bitches had done to me.

I knew in that moment that nothing would ever change. Not until I left.

Last year, I'd had hope that if I tried hard enough, I could fit in, make people forget why they hated me.

This year, I'd given up.

With a heavy heart, I rounded the corner, and Devilbend North High School came into view—patchy dry grass and cracked pavement framing the low brown building with bars over the windows.

I arrived with just enough time to go to my locker and get to my first class. Keeping my head down, my hair draped over the birthmarked side of my face, I sat off to the side about halfway back—not in the back with the assholes who thought they were cool and rebellious, and not in the front with the kids who were constantly called on to answer questions. I didn't speak to anyone or look at anyone who wasn't a teacher. I did my best to remain invisible, and I managed to get to lunch unnoticed and unscathed.

"Hi, Phil." Madison's voice was so close I almost flinched, but I somehow managed to calmly put my books away and close my locker, revealing her pretty, made-up face as she leaned on the lockers next to mine.

Kelsey was behind her, on her phone; the others milled about nearby, mostly ignoring me.

I turned to leave, but Steph and Bonnie blocked my path. Clearly they were paying more attention than I thought. I sighed and waited. The corridor was packed. They weren't above doing something mean to me in front of other people, but even they weren't stupid enough to pull a stunt as bad as the bathroom incident when teachers were close by.

"Where are you going? I'm just trying to say hi." Madison stepped around her friends to stand in front of me.

I kept my gaze on her purple kicks and said nothing.

After an extended silence, she leaned in and spoke low, close to my ear. "How was your summer?"

I kept my mouth shut. There was no right answer. If I replied, it would be thrown back in my face. If I tried to defend myself and was as much of a bitch to her as she was to *literally everyone else* . . . I shuddered to think.

"Nothing to say?" Madison tapped her foot as I remained still. "Good. We don't want a repeat of last year, do we? That bleach really fucked with my nails."

With a snicker, she led her sheep away, and I walked off in the opposite direction. At least we agreed on one thing—I didn't want a repeat of last year either.

I spent lunch in a back corner of the library. Food wasn't technically allowed in there, but if I was quiet enough between the bookshelves, no one noticed. I ate my sandwich as I scrolled through my Instagram feed, which was mostly filled with makeup pics and baby animals. I followed every person doing makeup I could find, but I never posted anything, and I had no followers. I was a lurker, too scared to post any of the hundreds of pics of my own makeup I had hidden on my phone.

Despite the horrible thing Madison and her friends had done to me, I hadn't abandoned my makeup hobby. There was something cathartic about focusing on a single task and being able to see the finished product— about pretending to be someone else for the few minutes before I wiped it all off again.

On my way out of the library, I heard that confident tone, the ocean-deep quality that wrapped around the smooth timbre of his words. For the first time that day, I lifted my head and looked for the guy I'd spent hours talking to on my balcony. The hallway was packed with students making their way to class, and I couldn't see him anywhere.

Then I rolled my eyes and remembered I had no idea what he looked like.

It was just my pathetic heart hoping against hope that I might have something positive at school for a change. I didn't even know if he went to school. He was probably older and way out of my league.

I dropped my gaze again and wished for a hoodie for the millionth time that day.

As I settled into my seat for my last class, I heard it again.

I was just reaching into my bag to grab my English textbook when that voice made me pause, hunched over, my hand tightening around the book's spine.

"Yeah, we moved to Devilbend last week," he said. There was no mistaking it this time. It was definitely Turner, and he was definitely walking right past my desk.

"Yeah, nice."

I clenched my teeth. *Jayden*. The only person who made my life hell as much as Madison.

"You gonna try out for the team?" Jayden asked.

"Which team?"

The two chairs in front of me scraped, and they sat down. I straightened and placed the book gently in front of me, keeping my eyes on the desk but straining to listen.

"Oh, yeah." Jayden laughed. "The football team."

"Yeah, I'll think about it." Turner sounded friendly, pleasant, like any guy having a normal conversation with a new person.

I chewed my lip to hold in the sigh, fighting to keep the scowl off my face.

Mr. Chen came in, demanding the class's attention, and Turner and Jayden stopped talking. When I was certain everyone's focus was on the front of the room, I slowly raised my eyes.

My heart thudded in my chest. He sat directly in front of me, Jayden on his left. There were those broad shoulders I'd seen only in silhouette, the white cotton of a collared T-shirt stretched over them. He had dark blond hair, cropped short at the base of his neck but wavy and growing just past his ears on the sides. He needed a haircut.

He reached up to scratch the back of his neck, and I nearly jumped as I looked away. But not before I noticed how long and strong his fingers looked, his nails square, the muscles in his arms flexing from the movement.

I made sure to look only directly at my desk and the teacher for the rest of the class, as I usually did. All I needed was for someone to notice me staring at the new guy.

It was lucky it was only the first day and we spent most of the class going over the syllabus, because I hardly heard a word Mr. Chen said.

I was in so much trouble.

CHAPTER 4

I WENT STRAIGHT TO THE BALCONY AFTER school, but he never showed up. It was probably for the best—I had no idea what to say. I just had an irresistible urge to speak to him.

I couldn't do it at school though—they'd find a way to ruin it. Of course, once he realized who I was, what I looked like, the flirting would stop, but I wanted to at least stay friends. That meant ignoring the fuck out of him at school and staying out of his way.

I still caught glimpses though. Anytime I heard his voice in the halls, I couldn't help looking up. He was friendly, talkative; I saw him chatting to several seniors and even a few juniors, but I never hung around long enough to hear the conversations.

He didn't come to the balcony for several nights, and I started to think maybe he'd already realized who I was. But that wasn't possible.

I was so determined to avoid him at school I didn't get a proper look at his face until my shift at the diner on

Wednesday night.

He came in with his dad—a taller, frownier version of Turner with gray hair at his temples. They sat in a booth, thankfully not in my section.

Chelsea took their order while I stared at the beautiful boy so clearly out of my league. He had that defined jaw—not square exactly, but strong—and a heavy brow. Gone was the smiling, open guy who talked to everyone at school. This Turner matched his dad's posture, leaning forward on the table with his shoulders hunched, his brow furrowed. I couldn't even tell what color his eyes were.

As soon as Chelsea walked away, they leaned back into each other, but not before Turner cast those dark eyes about the diner, as if checking for anyone listening in, or maybe looking for someone.

I turned away to clear a table.

"Philly, can you pour table three's coffees for me?" Chelsea caught me just as I unloaded a tray of dirty dishes. "I'm busting for the toilet."

She ran off without waiting for a response.

Shit. I picked up the coffee pot and swallowed around the ball of anxiety lodged in my throat. My gaze stayed on the ground as I approached their table.

". . . you sure?" Turner's dad's voice was as deep and gruff as it had been on the balcony the other night.

"Yeah, Dad. But it hasn't even been a week. I'm still learning the layout—" Turner cut himself off as I poured the coffee. He glanced up at me, my every nerve aware of him in my periphery as I hoped like hell my hand

43

wouldn't shake and spill coffee all over them.

"Thank you, miss." His dad gave me a small smile. I smiled back and nodded, the effort not to look at Turner directly almost crushing.

Then I walked away and avoided Chelsea until they left.

On Friday night, I walked out onto the balcony hardly even expecting him to be there. Maybe the feet smell had come back and they'd moved.

"Hello?"

His voice made me jump, my hand flying to my chest. "Fuck. You scared the crap out of me."

He chuckled. "Hey, neighbor."

I drew my cardigan closer, hunching against the light breeze, and smiled. "Hey, stranger."

"How was work?"

"How'd you know I was at work?" Had he seen me? Maybe heard me talking to another customer? Fuck!

"Uh . . . lucky guess? It's late and . . . I swear I'm not an axe murderer, Mena."

Oh god—my name on his lips, uttered so casually and confidently. I wanted him to end every sentence he spoke to me with my name.

"No, you're just a stalker, Turner."

He laughed lightly and shifted, knocking the bamboo screen. It was getting a little cold, but I moved the chair out of the way and sat next to him, against the wall.

"So? How was work?" he asked again. His light was off, and I couldn't even see his silhouette. I reached up and flicked my light off too. For some reason, it felt easier to say what I wanted to say in the dark.

"Work was fine. Same old." I chewed on my bottom lip and blurted it before I chickened out. "How was school? It can be hard being the new kid, but I have a feeling you're handling it just fine."

There was a beat of silence. My heart hammered in my chest, my throat, my whole damn body.

"Now who's the stalker?" He sounded amused, if a little wary.

"It's not stalking if I have a legitimate reason to be there."

"So, you go to Devilbend North High? What year are you in? Shit! Are you a teacher? I mean, not that it matters—to me. I wouldn't care. Although that would be technically illegal, I guess. But I am eighteen, if that makes any difference." As abruptly as he'd launched into his rambling, he cut himself off.

My head swam a little, even as the grin spread over my lips.

He cleared his throat. "Did I just make shit really awkward?"

"What would technically be illegal, Turner?" I wasn't sure why I was making this conversation even *more* awkward for him. Maybe I liked seeing a hint of him being just as nervous about this as me—at least in this moment. He was so damn confident and self-assured the rest of the time.

He took a deep breath—he was so close, just on the other side of the screen. "It's illegal for a teacher to have a relationship with a student, isn't it?"

"Is that what this is?"

"Maybe it's what it could be. Maybe it's what I'd like it to be."

So fucking confident. So *not* what I was or ever would be. My smile drained away along with any excitement I'd had about this conversation, leeching out of me and into the cold concrete under my ass. "You don't even know me."

"I know enough that I want to know more. Can I see you?" The bamboo screen shifted, his perfect fingers gripping the edge.

"No!" I shot my hand out and covered his, keeping the screen in place.

"Why?"

"I . . . I can't . . . you don't . . . I'm just not ready, OK?"

"I don't understand. Mena, are you OK? I was joking before, but are you actually a teacher at my school?"

"No. I'm a student."

The relief was palpable in his sigh. He released his grip on the screen only to push farther past it and take my hand.

As his perfect, warm fingers tangled with mine, he asked, "Mena, what's this about? Why don't you want me to know who you are?"

Because you'll stop talking to me. "It's complicated. I just want you to know me—the real me—before you know who I am."

After a beat of silence, we both chuckled.

"Yeah, that made more sense in my head than it did coming out of my mouth," I said, glad that some of the heavy tension had lifted. "Look, this is all pretty new, and I like you . . ."

I took a deep breath, hardly believing I'd been that honest with a boy about how I felt.

He jumped in before I could keep speaking. "I like you too. A lot."

I squeezed his hand, running my thumb up and down his, taking a moment to get my shit together while I jumped around and screamed on the inside like a fangirl at a BTS concert. "Enough to be patient with me? I know this is weird. I just . . . I think it could be kind of fun?"

"Easy for you to say. You're not the one being stalked by someone who's probably in the CIA."

I laughed. "I think you mean the FBI. The CIA isn't supposed to operate on home soil."

"Why do you know that? The evidence is mounting."

"A friend of mine said it a while back, and it just kind of stuck." Harlow spent so much time on the internet I wasn't entirely sure when she slept, but she was full of random-ass facts.

"Oh? And what—" A low thrumming noise cut Turner off. His hand tensed around mine as all the lights went out. "What the fuck?"

"Chill. The electricity just went out. Happens about once a month on this side of town—sometimes more often in the summer. The grid is old and unreliable. It'll be back up in ten minutes."

"Seriously? What a pain in the ass."

"You get used to it."

The sun had gone down an hour ago, and the night was overcast. Without the glow of the moon, it was pretty much pitch black. And I had at least five minutes before the lights came back on.

I extracted my hand from Turner's and got to my feet.

"Wait, Mena—"

"Shh!" With the electricity out, there was no background noise either. My parents were asleep, but we had to be extra quiet, just in case. "Stand up."

"Did you just shush me?" he whispered, sounding amused, but he shuffled and did as I asked.

I gripped the edge of the bamboo screen and unhooked it from the nails holding it to the wall. When I rolled it aside, there was nothing between us but the metal railing separating his side of the balcony from mine.

My eyes were adjusting to the heavy darkness, and I could just make out his silhouette. I reached out and tentatively placed my hand on his arm. It was ridiculously hard, like warm rocks under his skin.

He responded to my touch immediately, reaching out and placing his hands on my waist.

"Oh, hey, neighbor," he whispered, leaning in.

"Hey, stranger," I whispered back, moving my arms up to his shoulders. Why was every part of him so damn solid? And why did I want to run my hands over every inch of it? And why was being so close to him making a heavy, pressured feeling appear low in my belly? "I know we can't technically see each other, but I hope this makes up for it a bit."

His hands flexed, and we leaned into each other more.

"Yeah, this makes up for it." His breath fanned over my face. He was so close I could almost make out the lines of his jaw, his straight nose. But none of the details. And if I couldn't see the color of his eyes, I was pretty positive he couldn't see my birthmark.

My boobs pressed against his hard chest, and my breath hitched. He smelled like fresh rain and something warm and comforting—amber, maybe.

"Fuck, you smell good." *Zero filter*. I closed my eyes and cringed, but he just pulled me closer, his hands moving to my back, the railing digging into my hips. I hated that damn railing.

"You *feel* good. Can I kiss you?"

"Please . . ." I didn't even have time to consider how desperate I sounded. The word was barely out of my mouth before he closed the miniscule distance between our lips and kissed me firmly.

He sighed and moved his lips against mine in a determined but gentle way. His body was hard and lean, but his lips were pillow soft.

It didn't take long for the kiss to intensify. I don't know if he darted his tongue out or if I sucked on his bottom lip first, but then our tongues were involved, and little gasping breaths were coming out of my throat.

The thrum of the transformer on the corner

snapped me out of the moment, adrenaline coursing through my veins as surely as the electricity was rushing through the wires. I knew that sound—I had about five seconds before the lights turned back on.

"Fuck." I pulled away abruptly, and he grunted, his body following mine, his hands gripping my clothing.

"Shit. Sorry." He let go immediately, and I shoved his shoulders until he was safely on his side of the balcony. I yanked the bamboo screen across just as the streetlights below once again bathed the world in artificial light.

I chuckled through shaky breaths, the exhilaration of having kissed Turner, then gotten away with what I'd just pulled, still igniting my every nerve. "That was . . ."

"Yeah . . ." he breathed. "Are you sure you don't work for the CIA? That was a little too perfectly timed."

"FBI, remember? And I never denied it."

He laughed, his voice lower, huskier—it sent desire shooting through my body again. I wanted to feel his lips against mine as he made that sound; I wanted to feel it reverberate through his chest. I clenched my thighs, suddenly aware of the moisture in my underwear.

I had to get out of there before I broke down and did something stupid—like show him my face. "I have to get to bed."

"Wait." The urgency in his voice pulled me up short. He shuffled around for a moment, then shoved his hand through the narrow gap between the bamboo and the wall, his phone clutched in his perfect fingers. Fingers that had been digging into my back moments ago, holding me against him as he . . .

I shook my head. *Focus, Philomena!*

His screen displayed the keypad.

"You want my number?" I asked. "How . . . old school."

"I mean, I'm happy to connect on Insta or Snap or Twitter, or even Facebook, but you're determined to maintain your secret spy identity, and I'd like to talk to you outside of this balcony from time to time, so . . ." He wiggled the phone at me.

I took it and entered my number, saving it under "Neighbor." "Good night, Turner."

"Sweet dreams, Mena."

Naturally, I didn't sleep a wink that night. I'd never experienced such a high. Sure, I'd kissed a few guys before at some of Amaya's parties—I'd even liked one enough to get to second base with him in her pool house—but I'd never stayed up all night replaying every single thing a boy had said to me. Not to mention the kissing—*oh god*, the kissing!

Every time I thought about it, I either grinned or bit my lip to keep from making a frustrated/excited sound.

The pressure between my legs didn't abate—if anything, it intensified to a constant dull throb. I rolled onto my front and pressed my face into my pillow, dragging my hand down my body and between my legs as I imagined Turner's perfect, strong fingers pushing my panties aside. I was so worked up it didn't take long before I panted my release into my pillow, biting it to keep silent.

Only after that was I finally able to sleep.

The Turner-induced euphoria lasted well into the next day. It was harder than usual to keep my head down and avoid contact with everyone when all I wanted was to spread my arms wide and shout to the whole world how amazing he made me feel. I had to bite the inside of my cheek to keep myself from grinning when I passed him in the hall on the way to second period.

I was putting my books away in my locker at lunch, smiling as I thought of how his lips had felt against mine, when my locker door slammed shut. I flinched back, only narrowly avoiding getting my arm or head smacked by the metal.

My smile fell, all thoughts of Turner replaced by fear.

"What the fuck could you possibly have to smile about?" Jayden leaned against the locker next to mine, frowning as though he were doing long division without a calculator.

Jayden was Madison's boyfriend—as if that wasn't the most predictable fucking high school scenario. The mean girl dated the dumb jock, and they liked to make other people's lives miserable so they could feel better about themselves. *Groan.*

Jayden had started at DNHS the same day I had. We could've been friends—comrades in being the new kids at school. Madison had been a bitch to me from day one, making lame jokes about my birthmark that half the class laughed along with. Jayden had actually treated me like a human being for a few days. We had lunch together, shared awkward fourteen-year-old chitchat. Then one day I saw Madison and her friends talking to him at lunch. Then he tried out for the football team. Then he ignored me for a solid week. When he sat down next to me at lunch the following Monday, I was happy, excited to have my friend back.

"How was your weekend?" he'd asked.

I smiled and started to tell him, but he cut me off before I could get one word out. "Oh wait!" He half turned in his seat, and that's when I realized Madison and her friends were watching us, tittering on the sidelines. "I just remembered—I don't give a shit."

They all burst into laughter. Jayden's eyes flicked between what I'm sure was the devastated look in my eyes and the popular kids howling like hyenas. I guess that was his initiation—publicly making me feel like shit.

After that, Jayden and I settled into a new routine. I avoided him as much as all the other assholes, and he pretended I didn't exist in the most obnoxious and oxymoronic way possible. He routinely bumped into me and loudly said, "What was that? There's clearly nothing there, but I just tripped." Or he looked right through me and took a deep inhale, then said another moronic thing like "Do you guys smell that? I don't see anything, but something smells like *loser*." Naturally, everyone laughed at his brilliant jokes.

He'd spoken directly to me only a handful of times—

incidents I wished I could forget.

I fought to keep my breathing under control, focusing on a spot at the bottom edge of my locker where a bit of the bluish-gray paint had chipped off. Hoping he'd just go away.

He leaned in, his face close to my cheek, and said in a light, conversational tone, "I asked you a fucking question, Phil."

"Nothing," I replied as calmly as I could. *I* wasn't allowed to ignore *them*.

"That's right—you're nothing. You may as well not exist."

Then why are you talking to me, idiot? I so wished I was brave enough to say some of the things that went through my head.

Lucky for me, Jayden was easily distracted.

"Hey, new guy!" He turned away, relegating me back to phantom status.

"Hey, man."

Turner. I lifted my gaze toward the voice before I even knew what I was doing.

For one glorious, torturous moment, our eyes met. In a world where I was invisible, he looked directly at me and he saw me, a slight frown marring his strong brow. He'd saved me from whatever fucked-up thing Jayden had planned without even knowing it.

I looked away quickly as Jayden slung his arm over Turner's shoulders and led him away, leaning in to speak to him.

I grabbed my bag and beelined for the picnic table

at the back of the science building. It was in a dingy spot, and one of the benches was split, but no one ever went there. I sat down heavily and dropped my head on my arms, unable to eat the sandwich I'd made myself that morning.

The churning in my empty stomach persisted until school let out. As I trailed into the hot afternoon sun along with the other students, I once again spotted Turner. My heart stuttered, and I couldn't help slowing down. He looked so beautiful, his messy hair shining like gold in the sun, his broad shoulders relaxed, his brilliant smile wide.

But who was he smiling at? I frowned as Jayden thumped him on the back and Turner extended one hand.

The man standing with them was a little shorter than Jayden, but he had the same build, the same dark brown hair, the same olive complexion. His gray suit stretched over his back as he reached out to shake Turner's hand.

Why was Turner shaking hands with Jayden's dad? Why was the older man even here?

I couldn't hear what they were saying, but it looked harmless enough. Except I knew how rotten Jayden was deep down. Could the rancid apple really have fallen that far from the tree?

Before I could move closer to listen in, Jayden happened to look over and spot me. His already tight smile fell into a frown, the look one of pure derision, and I realized I was blatantly staring.

I dropped my head and rushed in the opposite direction of home, resigned to taking the long way back—just in case Turner saw me and got suspicious.

I had to be more careful. Meeting Turner was the best thing that had happened to me in a long time—I couldn't risk any of the assholes at school finding out and ruining it.

CHAPTER 5

THERE WERE ABOUT TEN MINUTES LEFT UNTIL lunch ended, and I resisted the urge to text Turner. We'd exchanged numbers a week ago, but I was keeping the texting strictly to outside of school. God forbid anyone notice me interacting with another human being. We talked every night though, if not on the balcony then on the phone.

He kept asking when he could see me again, and I kept deflecting with coyness and jokes about keeping the mystery alive, but I knew this would have to come to a head eventually. He'd probably lose interest before I got up the courage to show him who I really was.

I sighed and drew my knees up, leaning my head on the row of encyclopedias as I opened Instagram to distract myself. I was studying a makeup look with a watercolor effect on the eyes, wondering which products the artist had used, when I heard my name.

"Mena, Mena, Mena." It was barely a whisper, but it was definitely Turner's voice. How the fuck had he figured out who I was?

Eyes wide, I looked around, but all I could see were the rows of books on the shelves to either side of me and a cart at the end of the row I was hiding out in.

Fuck, was I starting to hallucinate?

"Middle name?" he mumbled, sounding more confused. His voice was coming from my right.

Slowly, as soundlessly as possible, I lifted onto my knees and peered through the narrow, uneven gap in the books.

He was standing on the other side; my eyes were about level with the top button of his jeans. Twisting my head, I could just see the bottom of last year's yearbook as he slowly turned the pages and cursed under his breath.

I covered my mouth to hold back my laughter. He was trying to figure out who I was, sweet, infuriating boy.

Balancing the yearbook on one hand, he reached the other above his head and leaned on the bookshelf. His T-shirt rode up, revealing his hips, the toned muscles in his lower abdomen, the trail of light hair disappearing into the top of his jeans. I had an urge to shove all the books out of the way so I could run my hands through that hair, maybe lick one of the hipbones peeking out next to it.

"Hey, bro!" Jayden's voice was like a bucket of icy water poured over my head. I recoiled and barely caught myself before I smacked into the opposite bookshelf.

"Hey, Jayden." Turner sounded friendly, but I knew

his voice—there was a hint of annoyance there too.

"What the fuck are you doing in the library?" Jayden laughed, as though the very existence of libraries was preposterous. I allowed myself an eye roll.

"Some of us know how to read." Turner's voice was light, as if he was laughing *with* Jayden and not *at* him. I still wanted to kiss him for the dig at that asshole's intelligence.

"Fuck you, asshole." Jayden laughed, not sounding the least bit offended. "Come on, I've been looking for you. Coach wants to talk to you."

I heard the yearbook getting shoved back into place, and then they started to walk away. I frowned. Turner hadn't mentioned anything to me about who he was making friends with at school, but if he started hanging out with them, that would really fucking suck. Couldn't he see how fake and mean they were? I wasn't the only student at DNHS whose life was made miserable because of those dicks.

I was just the only one who wasn't allowed to make friends with other misfits—because I didn't exist or matter, as they liked to remind everyone.

I sat back on my heels and tried to quell the panic. Maybe if I came clean now, told him who I was and how they treated me . . . but what if he thought I was pathetic and stopped talking to me? What if he already knew and was just in on some elaborate prank?

I squeezed my eyes shut and tried to push that last thought out of my mind—it was too painful.

"Hey, pipsqueak." Jayden's voice sounded farther

away, but it still made me open my eyes, my body primed to go on the alert at any sign of him. "Dad's picking you up after school, so don't waste time after the last bell, all right?"

A small voice murmured in response, and then the sound of the library doors opening and closing announced that they'd left.

A moment later, a skinny girl rounded the corner. She saw me sitting on the ground and froze, clutching her open bag to her chest. She was clearly a freshman. She had that deer-in-the-headlights look that starting high school put in everyone's eyes. Her dark blonde hair was cut short, and she had knobby knees under her cute blue shorts. When she grew out of this awkward stage, she'd be gorgeous. And since she was Jayden's sister, she'd probably be a total bitch too.

Jayden had never mentioned having a sister, but we were friends for only a grand total of three days, and I'd been avoiding him like the plague ever since.

"Did you drop something?" her soft voice asked, even as she averted her gaze.

"Huh?" I frowned, then remembered I was sitting on the ground. "Oh, yeah, kind of." My dignity. My sanity. My sense of self-preservation.

I shoved my phone and the remnants of my lunch into my bag, rose up onto my knees, but paused before I fully got to my feet.

The girl had buried her chin in her chest, and her eyes were watering, seconds away from spilling fat tears down her innocent cheeks.

"Hey, what's wrong?" I shuffled forward, the worn carpet scratchy against my bare knees.

She shook her head. "Nothing."

I took a chance and placed a gentle hand on her shoulder. She jumped slightly at the contact but didn't shrug me off. "Doesn't look like nothing."

She took a lightning-quick glance at me. Whatever she saw must've been enough to crack her defenses just a little more.

"It's just ..." She breathed hard, and the tears spilled over. "It's just overwhelming. I feel like I'm drowning, and I don't know what to do."

I sighed. I didn't want to feel anything for anyone even remotely related to Jayden, but she was so vulnerable, so broken. "I get it. Starting high school can be hella scary. Everyone feels like this from time to time, OK? Even if they don't show it. It does get better."

It hadn't gotten better for me. It got worse. But she didn't need to hear that. She just needed someone to tell her it would be OK.

She bit her lip. If anything, she looked sadder, but her tears were drying up.

"What's your name?" I asked, rubbing her shoulder lightly.

"Jenny," she mumbled, her voice a little steadier.

"Hang in there, Jenny." I gave her a reassuring smile. "You can do this."

She met my eyes. She didn't smile back, but she did give a little nod.

The bell rang, and her eyes widened. "I can't be late."

She zipped up her bag, swung it onto her back, and turned to rush away.

I grabbed my own bag and got to my feet just in time for her to turn back and wrap her gangly arms around my waist.

"Thank you," she mumbled into my T-shirt, then ran off before I even had a chance to hug her back.

I saw her again at the end of the day, along with another, unfortunately familiar, face. I didn't know what it was about Jayden's dad—I hadn't even met him—but I'd taken an immediate dislike to him, probably because he was related to Jayden. Or maybe I was just jealous that he could stand in front of the school and shake hands with Turner in front of everyone, while I had to keep my very identity secret from the boy I liked.

As I made my way through the parking lot, I watched him out of the corner of my eye. He was leaning against his car and reading something on his phone when Jenny walked up. She reached for the car door, but he stopped her so he could grab something off the front seat. Bending at the waist until they were at eye level, he pulled a cupcake out of a paper bag and held it out with a big smile.

She was facing away from me, so I didn't see the happiness the sugary treat surely brought to her face.

Maybe I'd misjudged Mr. Burrows after all.

When was the last time my parents got me a cupcake for no reason, let alone picked me up from school? I had to walk even when it was pouring down rain. It wasn't their fault—they both worked hard—but still, it wasn't fair.

Jayden bumped my shoulder, nearly making me drop my bag, as he barrelled past me toward his family.

I turned and hastened away, both happy the sad little girl was having her day brightened and bitter that an asshole like Jayden had anything positive in his life. Why shouldn't he suffer the same way he made me suffer every day?

After school, I needed to focus on something other than Turner, so I got my makeup out with the intention of trying to re-create that watercolor look I'd seen on Instagram. I quickly realized I didn't have the right kind of eyeshadow and decided to do a dramatic vintage look with killer winged eyeliner instead.

It had been a dramatic day, so it was only fitting.

With a full face of makeup, I spread my books out on my bed and started on my homework. I worked on an English essay, then reluctantly moved on to a Statistics worksheet.

Halfway through my fourth question—and about fifty percent sure the previous three were wrong anyway—the sound of the front door opening provided the perfect excuse to stop.

I stretched my arms over my head and walked into the kitchen to find my mom depositing several grocery bags on the counter.

"Hey, Mom. Is Dad working late?" They both picked up overtime whenever it was offered. That usually resulted in takeout for dinner—my parents liked to cook together as they talked about their day. I used to sit at the dining table and do my homework, or when I was little, they'd give me something nonessential to the meal to chop.

"Yeah." She smiled at me, then paused. "Oh my god, Philomena, you look stunning! When did you grow up?"

She stroked a lock of hair hanging over my shoulder as she inspected my makeup.

"Thanks, Mom." She was so busy, so overworked and tired, it was rare for us to talk like this.

"I'm making pulled pork tacos for dinner. Wanna help?"

I shot her a skeptical look. She was full of energy and in a suspiciously good mood, but it was nice, so I chose not to question it. "Fine. But only because you buttered me up with your compliments."

"Great! Can you unload while I freshen up? Thanks!" She didn't wait for a response before disappearing into the bathroom.

"Child labor . . ." I grumbled as I started putting things away.

She came back in a pair of my sweats, her hair up in a messy bun and her contacts replaced with glasses. We were the same size, but my mom was a little shorter.

Mom chatted about her work, the gossip she'd heard from the ladies she had coffee with every Saturday afternoon, and the movie she'd fallen asleep during the other night. She asked a few questions about school and my friends, but I'd perfected dodging those questions a long time ago. Instead I told her about the math homework I was struggling with and the few things I did with my cousins and Amaya.

My parents had enough on their plate without worrying about me. What would be the point in telling them I didn't have any friends at school? They couldn't afford to send me to Fulton Academy, and there were no other public schools I could get to in under an hour on public transport. I was better off gritting my teeth and getting through it. Not counting days off, I had only 174 days of school to go. I was on the home stretch.

"You know what we haven't done in a long time?" Mom said as we laid everything out on the table. "A girls' day with your aunt Emily and your cousins."

I smiled. "Yeah, we should definitely organize that."

When we moved back to Devilbend, my mom and her sister had started organizing girls' days for us. My mom hadn't really kept in touch with my aunt before we moved back—I wasn't sure why—but Auntie Em seemed really happy to have us living so close. She invited us over all the time and had encouraged us girls to become friends.

We'd go to parks and have picnics, go for hikes, or even take the hour-and-a-half drive into San Francisco and spend the day there—although my mom didn't like that too much; it was expensive. I didn't see what the issue was when my aunt was happy to pay for everything.

"That smells amazing." My dad toed his shoes off at the door, back just in time for dinner.

"Gross!" I gagged as my mom gave him a big hug and kiss.

We sat at the dining table to eat for the first time in weeks, and the TV even stayed off. Dad was exhausted, but Mom was in the best mood I'd seen her in for a long time. I figured it had something to do with a class she kept rambling on about. It was run by BestLyf—I knew nothing about them other than that they had a tall building in downtown Devilbend and employed a lot of people from the nicer side of town—and Mom had attended her first session over the weekend. It sounded like self-help bullshit and was likely to go the route of the yoga class she'd taken at the community center, or the pottery class she'd taken with Auntie Em, or the stack of adult coloring books she'd brought home one time. None of those things had lasted, but they'd each given her a brief period of excited energy.

When I went back to my room, my math homework was still sitting on my bed, mocking me in all its half-finished glory. I sent Turner a text whining about it and then packed up all the books, deciding to get up early and finish it tomorrow.

After sending the girls a pic of my makeup, I headed to the bathroom to wash it all off and get ready for bed.

I got a little pang of excitement when I returned to see my phone flashing with notifications. I didn't get a lot of messages. Usually it was Mom or Dad telling me they were working late or asking me to do a chore.

I turned the light off, got into bed, propped my phone on my pillow, and settled in for some scrolling before trying to sleep.

The messages were from the girls, gushing about how good I looked and how flawless my makeup was. Amaya begged me to post them on Instagram every single time I sent a pic, and tonight was no different.

In between chatting with them, I scrolled Instagram, obsessing over makeup that was way better than what I could do and trying to ignore the fact that Turner still hadn't replied.

Under a pic of some artfully arranged makeup brushes, there was a post from the "DNHS Confessions Page."

"The new guy—Turner—is fucking hot!"

Usually I scrolled past, trying not to read what they said, but Turner's name caught my attention. Like a masochist, I tapped on the page and scrolled through the recent confessions. No one knew who ran the page, but the description read, "Send us your Devilbend North High tea, and we'll spill it for you! Oops!" Students sent in anonymous comments, gossip, and bitchy things, and the page posted them all, unedited. I had a feeling Kelsey ran it. Something like that would require someone mean-hearted to keep it going, and that bitch was always on her phone.

There were several posts about how hot Turner was and what people wanted to do to him. There were common ones like "Anna cheated on the science quiz" or "Meg and Josh were making out in the back of the admin building even though Josh has a girlfriend." The juicy gossip was interspersed with just plain *mean* comments.

At least one per day was about me. "Phil looks particularly fat today," "Is that thing on her face contagious?" and so on. It was a running joke for people to then comment with some variation of "Who? What are you talking about?"

I growled and locked the screen, dropping the phone on the bed beside me and rolling onto my back.

Why was I reading that shit? Why was I doing that to myself?

Those people weren't my friends. I didn't like them, and they definitely didn't like me. But it still hurt to read comment after comment about how fucking worthless I was as a human being.

I'd tried to switch off from it completely once. I deactivated my accounts and embraced being as invisible as they all liked to joke I was. It was bliss . . . for about two days. Then I opened my locker at school, and a sea of paper came flying out. Hundreds of printouts of posts, comments, and taunts I'd avoided while offline smacked me in the face, quite literally.

"We saw you deactivated your accounts, and we didn't want you to miss anything important," Kelsey had said, a self-satisfied smile on her face.

"Can't believe you're going to keep killing trees when you can read all this online. Don't you know we're in a climate crisis?" Madison's threat had been clear— get back online or keep receiving printouts.

Defeated, I cleaned up the mess before one of them reported it to a teacher and got me in trouble. Then I reactivated my accounts. What else could I do?

And if I really thought about it, I'd missed the makeup accounts I followed, not to mention talking to the only people my age who didn't treat me like shit—the girls.

My phone vibrated next to my thigh, and I picked it up reflexively, my heart kicking up a notch, as it did every time. I never knew if the notification would bring a mundane message from one of my parents or an anonymous suggestion I end my own life.

It was Turner.

> **Turner:** Sorry I didn't reply sooner. It's been a crazy day. I had to help my dad with something. Did you get the math homework done?

I smiled and responded immediately, not even caring if that looked as if I'd been up just staring at my phone, waiting for him to message me. I was so happy to hear from him.

CHAPTER 6

I POURED SALT INTO THE SHAKER AND PASSED IT to Chelsea. She screwed the top on while I did the next one, both of us taking our time, leaning on the end of the counter.

Barry, the cook, was out back having a break, and Leah had taken the night off. Tuesday nights were always quiet, so a good part of my shift was spent refilling the salt, pepper, and sugar shakers and restocking the takeaway cups, along with general cleaning and tidying. And of course, gossiping with Chelsea. Or rather she'd gossip, talking a million miles an hour, while I dropped in the occasional "OMG!" or "Are you serious?"

She used to talk a lot about her boyfriend and his friends, but they'd broken up recently, and now she talked more about some new course she wanted to do.

"Sorry, what was it called?" I realized I'd zoned out and overfilled the last saltshaker. I mopped up my mess as she repeated what she'd been saying.

"BestLyf." She huffed. I was pretty sure that was the same thing my mom had been talking about the other day. "You OK, girl? You seem more quiet than usual. Distracted."

"Yeah, I'm fine. Sorry. Just tired." I'd been staying up way too late talking to Turner on the balcony or on the phone. I gave her a smile, and she launched right back in.

"Well, remember the info session I mentioned a couple of weeks ago?" She waved the saltshaker lid around animatedly as she talked.

"Uh-huh." I nodded and glanced around the diner, making sure the three currently occupied tables didn't need anything.

"Well, it was so good. I mean, I only went because I had nothing better to do, and that chick I met at yoga was raving about it, and she seemed nice, but it was totally worth it. They even had sushi platters out after, and I didn't have to worry about dinner." She chuckled, and I gave her a wide smile. That girl was obsessed with raw fish. "It was the first time in, like, a month I managed to not think about Dave for more than ten fucking minutes." At the mention of her ex, her face fell.

I dropped the large box of salt and squeezed her hand. "He didn't deserve you."

"No, he did not." She squared her shoulders, and we got back to work. "I mean, I came out here for him. I left all my friends and my family back in Illinois because I thought we were in love and creating a life together. Then six months after we move here, he dumps me and moves to San Francisco! He is such a fucking asshole."

I shushed her, glancing around at the patrons again.

She cringed. "Sorry. Anyway, I've been thinking about moving to San Fran myself, just to stick it to him, ya know? But it's so expensive. And then I was thinking about moving home, but I haven't told my mom that we broke up yet, and I've kinda lost touch with my friends and . . . I dunno. Anyway, I think I'm gonna stay now. That info session really helped put things in perspective for me. I learned that it's OK to put myself and my happiness first, so that's what I'm gonna do."

"You learned all that from one free info session? Wow."

"No, silly." She grinned. We finished with the salt and moved on to the sugar. "I've been to three free info sessions, and the other night I went to my first workshop, which they charge for, but it was so worth it."

"You went to four events in two weeks?" I asked, a little surprised.

"Yeah! I mean, it's not like I had anything better to do, and I was learning so much and meeting all these amazing, successful people. I think it's lucky that BestLyf has one of its centers right here in Devilbend. Makes it possible for them to offer more events, ya know?"

"Uh-huh. Lucky. I'm really happy for you, Chelsea. It's good to see you so positive again." I didn't know much about this program, but I wanted to be supportive.

"Thank you." She beamed. "Hey, you should come. They're super welcoming to everyone. It's a really flexible program that's tailored to your individual needs, the further along you get. The main focus is always on helping you be your best self—whatever that means for you."

"Uh, yeah, maybe . . ."

The bell above the door dinged, saving me from having to awkwardly avoid going to whatever motivational self-help crap Chelsea had gotten involved in.

"I got it." I rushed to the door before she could say anything else.

Donna, Harlow, and Amaya walked in wearing their school uniforms, looking cute in their knee-high socks and so pretty. I'd never look that pretty. The table of college guys in the corner watched them with unconcealed interest.

"Well, hello there, fair maidens." I gave them a mock bow. "Welcome to our humble establishment. How may I be of service this evening?"

Donna and Amaya chuckled, but Harlow jumped right into the ridiculousness with me. "Your finest table, wench. We're weary travelers in need of a warm meal to fill our bellies and a pitcher of your best mead."

"Who you callin' wench, bitch?" I dropped the act and stepped forward to give them each a hug before leading them to a booth.

"That uniform looks amazing on you." Amaya tugged on the edge of my stained blue apron.

I gave her a skeptical look. "Please."

"I'm serious. The apron cinches you in at the waist

and accentuates your curves. I'd kill for half your boobs." She grabbed her own admittedly smaller boobs and looked down at her modest cleavage. The table of college guys started squawking and carrying on, nudging each other like a flock of seagulls.

We all rolled our eyes at them.

"What are you guys doing here?" I asked, changing the topic.

"We went shopping after school and thought we'd grab dinner before heading home," Donna said, perusing the menu.

"Oh, OK. What can I get you?" I pulled my pen and pad out of my apron pocket, fighting to keep my smile from shaking. I knew they did things without me, had their own lives—how could they not when we went to different schools and had other social circles? Or rather, *they* had other people they hung out with. I was just alone all the time. It still hurt to be reminded of it.

"You mentioned you were working tonight, so we thought we'd come see you," Harlow added. My smile became more genuine.

"I'll have the cheeseburger with a side of fries and a strawberry milkshake, and do you guys wanna share the loaded nachos?" Amaya looked up to find us all staring at her. "What?" She dropped the menu and crossed her arms. "I'm fucking hungry."

I had no idea how that amount of food would even fit into her tiny stomach, but I recovered first. "Hey, no judgment. The nachos are really good."

The others ordered, and Donna asked when my

break was. I put their order in and, when it was ready, told Chelsea I was taking my break and went to sit with them for a little while.

I stole some of their nachos, Amaya playfully batting my hand back, but the ding of the bell over the door yanked my attention away.

Jayden's dad walked into the diner in a suit but no tie, the top few buttons of his shirt undone. He was off the clock.

He paused at the door and scanned the room, then smiled and walked forward when he spotted someone. *Chelsea.* I frowned, completely tuning out the girls as I focused on their exchange.

She smiled widely, as if he'd just handed her a million dollars and not a folded-up scrap of paper. She slipped the paper into her apron pocket, and they spoke briefly before Boyd extended his hand. Chelsea took it, and he covered her hand with his other one, holding on for an inappropriately long time while leaning in to speak into her ear.

Then, as unexpectedly as he'd appeared, he walked back out the door.

What the hell was going on? Was Chelsea having an affair with Jayden's dad? My stomach rolled at the thought. He was at least fifteen years older than her, but it would explain her sudden good mood and positive outlook. Was he even married though? I'd never cared to learn about Jayden's family life.

"Earth to Mena!" Harlow waved a hand in front of my face as the others laughed.

"Huh? Sorry!" I snapped out of it. I had enough problems of my own to worry about, and I didn't want to waste what time I had left with my friends thinking about anyone with the last name Burrows.

We talked shit, discussed the latest episode of the webtoon we were all reading, ranked the college guys in order of hotness. My break was over way too soon, but it was nice to spend time with them and feel normal for half an hour.

"I would've said to just hang out with your friends, Philly, but ..." Chelsea smiled apologetically as she picked up two plates from the servery.

"It's all good." I waved her off. A few more people had come in for dinner, and we really couldn't slack off anymore.

The girls hung around a bit longer, then came to say goodbye when there was a lull.

"It was so nice to see you guys." I held on to them each a little longer than I had saying hello. I hated saying goodbye, even though I knew I didn't mean as much to them as they meant to me.

"Same. Come over on the weekend." Harlow bounced on the spot, her big headphones jostling on her chest.

"Yeah, we can have another pool sesh before the weather turns to shit." Donna rolled her eyes.

"I gotta work." I huffed. The weather was already getting cold. Fall was beginning to turn the leaves golden, and I needed a cardigan to sit out on the balcony in the evenings.

"What about during the week?" Amaya asked.

"Homework, and I don't have a car . . ." I couldn't get to their place on the nice side of town without a car, and my parents were never home early enough to drive me.

"God, I keep forgetting. I'm such a bitch." Donna looked guilty. "We'll come pick you up one night. We'll sort it out later, OK? Get back to work."

"Sounds good. I can tell you about this guy I've been talking to."

"What?!" Amaya stopped midturn and faced me again. "Way to bury the lede."

"Yeah, we've been here all night, and you only mention this now?" Harlow whacked me on the arm.

Donna's eyes just sparkled, her smile brilliant and greedy. She wagged a finger in my face. "You're not getting away with this. There will be questions, missy. So many questions."

"And I will provide answers," I promised. "But I really gotta get back to work. Bye!"

I rushed away without waiting for a response. When I looked over my shoulder, Donna was dragging the other two out the door as they glared at me.

I held in a laugh and went to clear a table. It was nice to have them so interested in something going on with me—even if it was more because of the boy-related gossip than anything else. But as my shift came to a close, I started to worry about what exactly I would tell them. "Oh, I started talking to him on my balcony, and he goes to my school, and I've seen him (he's really hot,

BTW—way out of my league), but he has no idea what *I* look like. Also, we've kissed. Also, I'm pretty sure I'm falling in love with him."

Fuck my life . . .

* * *

The next time I saw Turner, the sight of his broad shoulders, encased in a dark gray hoodie, stopped me in my tracks before I made it around the corner. I'd spent so much time silently observing him I'd know his build, his mannerisms, anywhere.

I just wasn't expecting to see him at the bottom of the back stairs in the dingy end of the English and humanities wing. The last two classrooms had busted windows or other issues and weren't even used. I went out of my way to take these stairs from time to time to avoid bumping into Madison and her friends, or Jayden and his friends. I could count on one hand the number of people I'd seen in this part of the school.

"Just tell me what to do to prove . . . please!" I missed half of what he said as I silently plastered myself against the wall, tightly gripping the strap of my bag.

I was about to walk away, risk the main stairs, but the desperation in his voice kept me glued to the spot.

". . . that simple." The small voice that responded was female. Now I *definitely* wasn't going anywhere.

"OK, then how about—" Turner's ocean-deep voice had some ripples in it now, but a sharp shush cut him off.

He resumed talking, but I couldn't make out what he was saying.

I chewed on my bottom lip and tried to make myself walk away, but curiosity got the better of me. I took a deep breath and leaned around the corner.

Turner had shifted against the railing, revealing the person beyond: the sad little girl from the library the other day.

Jayden's little sister? *What the actual fuck?*

He was holding his hands out, palms up, as if he was pleading with her . . . or maybe threatening her? Her arms were wrapped around her waist, her head hanging. She looked so vulnerable—especially next to Turner's height and strength. He was easily twice her size.

Why the hell was he talking to a freshman in an abandoned part of the school, making her look as though she might burst into tears at any moment?

It killed me to even consider that the sweet, funny guy I was falling for wasn't who I thought he was, but I couldn't just stand there and do nothing . . . even though that's what all my classmates had done for years as I'd endured Madison's and Jayden's torture.

I was about to bust my cover. He'd know who I was as soon as I opened my mouth. He'd had nothing to focus on but my voice for weeks.

I didn't care.

I took a step around the corner, but Turner beat me to it. He leaned down and whispered something to Jenny, his big hand engulfing her delicate shoulder, then rushed away up the stairs.

Jenny lifted her face to the ceiling and sighed, unshed tears glistening on her lashes. She lowered her head and immediately spotted me.

Her eyes widened in fear—of me? Of him?

With one hand still gripping the strap of my bag, I cautiously reached the other out to her, taking small measured steps forward. "Hey, Jenny. Remember me? We met in the library the other day."

She nodded and glanced at the stairs. The tears spilled over.

"I just want to make sure you're OK. That looked kind of intense, and—"

"I'm fine," she interrupted, squaring her shoulders and swiping at the tears on her face. "Just leave me alone."

She started to move past me, and I let her, not wanting to make her feel any less safe.

"Was that guy bothering you?" That made her stop and face me again. "Did he do something to hurt you? Is he—"

"No," she interrupted me again. "Leave him alone too. He's just . . . just don't say anything to anyone, OK? It'll only make everything worse. I just . . . I need to think."

She rushed off, leaving me standing at the bottom of the stairs, confused.

She'd seemed afraid of him when they were talking, but I'd caught only a glimpse of it. Was she just upset? Maybe he was trying to comfort her? He did look as though he was pleading with her at one point. And the way she demanded I leave him alone . . . it was fiercer than the way she'd defended *herself*.

Was I reading this all wrong? Or was my connection with Turner making me search for any explanation that put him in a positive light?

CHAPTER 7

MOM AND DAD WERE BOTH WORKING LATE, AND I didn't even attempt to do any homework when I got home. I dumped my bag at the foot of my bed and immediately reached for my makeup case. I needed to clear my head, calm my racing heart, get lost in the precision and focus required to execute a full face of makeup.

I set up in my room, retrieving the circle light I'd had out on the balcony all summer. It was getting too cold to sit out there at night anyway, but really, I was avoiding Turner. My phone had lit up with several messages from him, and it took a Herculean effort not to read them. In the end, I put the damn thing on silent and shut it in my bedside drawer.

I ended up doing a split-face makeup—definitely not something you'd ever wear in public but fun to experiment with. One side was fierce, with a strong brow and smoky eye, a defined deep red lip, and contouring around the cheeks—the bitch you didn't mess with. The other half was youthful and vulnerable, with light makeup around the eyes, soft blush on the cheeks, and a gloss on the lips—the naïve young girl who needed protecting.

I was neither.

I was both.

It spoke to my confusion and conflicting feelings about the day.

I snapped a few photos and wiped it all off just before my dad walked through the front door. While he was in the shower, I started dinner, needing something to occupy my hands and my mind.

"Er . . . you feeling OK, Sweet Chilly?" He eyed the knife in my hand with wide eyes.

I gave him a withering look and got back to chopping the pepper. "Stir-fry, right?"

"I was gonna say we should get a pizza since your mom and I both worked late, but you've already done half the work, so sure!"

He put the rice on, and we had dinner ready in no time. Dad chattered about mundane things, asking about school and work. I managed to respond just enough to show I was listening, but half my mind was still in that stairwell with Turner and Jenny, my gut churning about what I'd seen and heard.

Obviously, I wasn't the only one with secrets. I just couldn't figure out if his were going to get me into trouble.

To both my parents' astonishment, I sat on the couch with them and watched some TV for a while, then

I went to bed early.

I took time with my evening routine before flopping into bed on my back, staring at the dark ceiling. With nothing left to distract me, I could no longer resist the urge to reach into my drawer and check my phone.

There were forty-eight messages in the group chat with the girls, mostly demands for more information about "the hottie you mentioned the other day."

An anonymous message told me I'd looked like shit today and should stop making other people deal with having to look at me by just killing myself. I got out of that one quickly, but my heart still plummeted in my chest.

There were three from Turner.

The first was from barely an hour after school.

Turner: Hey, neighbor. Balcony?

The second was from about half an hour later.

T: Mena? I didn't think you were working tonight. I miss you.

The third was sent about fifteen minutes ago.

T: Are you OK?

Was I? I supposed I was physically OK. Mentally, I was a confused mess. Emotionally? I didn't even know where to start.

I stared at my phone, trying to think of something to say until it went dark and locked itself. I groaned and ran my hand through my hair, then rolled onto my side, unlocked it, and replied.

Mena: I'm fine. Just need to think.

His reply was instant.

T: About? Anything I can help with?

My fingers hovered over the keyboard, my gut churning. What was I supposed to say? *Hey, are you doing something shady with Jayden's little sister?* It sounded insane, even in my own head, but I knew what I'd seen. I couldn't just ignore it.

On the other hand, if there was a logical explanation and I accused him of doing something awful, I'd feel really bad.

Every time we spoke, Turner seemed to me like a good person—I just couldn't reconcile that with how scared Jenny had looked while talking to him.

My screen went dark again, and he sent another message before I could.

T: Shit. Is it about me? About us?

M: Kind of. I don't really know how to explain it.

T: Fuck, Mena, what did I do? Did I say

85

something bad? The more I get to know
you, the less filter I have.

M: No, you didn't say anything or do anything
to me.

But what did you do to her?

T: Then what is it? Can we talk out on the
balcony? I want to hear your voice.

M: My parents just went to bed. I can't.

T: Then can I call you?

Without waiting for a response, he did. I let it ring
out and then replied.

M: They'll hear me. I can't talk to you right now.
I just need to process some things.

T: I can't fix anything if you don't tell me what
the issue is.

M: I don't know if this can be fixed.

T: Fuck. You're really scaring me.

M: I'm sorry. I'll talk to you tomorrow. I need to get some sleep.

He didn't reply for a long time. All I could think about was him in his bed, staring at his phone. Was he confused? Angry? Scared? Pissed off?

Maybe all of those things. I knew I was.

When he finally did respond, it was a simple "OK."

I put my phone away and rolled onto my other side, facing the wall, as tears pricked the backs of my eyes. He was the best thing that had happened to me in a long time. But was he who I thought he was? Or was I so desperate for human interaction that I was seeing something that wasn't there?

* * *

The next morning, I looked more like shit than usual. The lack of sleep and crying had left my eyes puffy and my nose red; even my birthmark looked worse.

Some concealer would've covered the imperfections, and a swipe of mascara would've made my eyes look more open and alert. But I just looked wistfully at my makeup case and remembered how scratchy the fibers of that mop had felt and how the smell of bleach had choked me, and I settled for washing my face with cold water, hoping that would bring the swelling down.

Like every morning, I drank my coffee on the

balcony and waited for Turner. He left later than usual—I guessed he hadn't slept much either—his shoulders hunched, hood up, hands in pockets.

I waited until he was around the corner, then I left, pulling my own hood up and tucking my ponytail out of the way.

Most of the day passed in a blur as I went from class to class, took scattered notes that would probably make no sense later, and avoided Turner in the halls. I'd figured out his schedule—or at least which general area of the school he would be in at any point in the day. Usually I used this information to pass him in the hall, get a glimpse of him, hear his smooth, deep voice as he talked.

Today, I used it to keep as far away from him as possible.

Even Bonnie bumping into me and loudly declaring, "That was weird. I just knocked into thin air. Does anyone see anything?" didn't make me feel as shitty as it usually did. A bunch of kids laughed as I walked away, but my mind was with Turner.

By lunch, my stomach was still churning, which meant I wasn't even remotely hungry. But I was over feeling like shit.

School was shitty enough. I couldn't have this hanging over my head too.

I sat down in the abandoned stairwell where I'd seen Turner talking to Jenny and got out my phone to text him.

He beat me to it.

T: Can we please talk? This is killing me.

M: Yes. I was just about to text you.

T: In person. Please. I want to talk to you.

M: Tonight? Balcony?

T: I can't tonight. My dad needs me. Can I come meet you somewhere? Please, Mena!

M: Lunch is half-over. There's no time.

T: I don't care. Can't fucking concentrate on anything anyway.

M: Me neither . . .

I chewed my bottom lip and racked my brain. I wasn't ready for him to see me, but I needed to speak to him. I craved his touch, even as I worried it might burn me.

It would have to be somewhere dark.

The gym would be empty during lunch. We'd have to finish our talk before the next class came in to use it.

> **M:** Meet me in the gym. There's a storage room at the back next to the seating. We should have privacy there.

I grabbed my bag, rushing in that direction as fast as I could. I should've waited until I was there before sending that text. Hopefully I could get there first.

The gym was empty, and I ran across the polished floor to the back corner, praying the door to the storage room would be unlocked. Luck was on my side, and the heavy door opened.

I dashed inside and took a deep breath.

Sneakers squeaked on the polished gym floor. I'd only just beaten him. Had he been close by? Or had he rushed here like me?

It was pitch black in the dank space, but light would flood it as soon as he opened the door. I hurried toward the other end of the room and around the corner, darting past the industrial shelving that held balls and mats and other torture devices high school gym teachers had used since time immemorial. The room was an L shape, with another door leading outside, providing access to the equipment from the football field.

The door opened. Light streamed in. I held my breath. What if it wasn't him?

"Mena?" he whisper-shouted into the room.

"Shut the door," I said. "Quick."

He closed the door, then cursed. "Where's the light?"

"No!" I stepped in his direction. "Just leave it. Come toward me."

"Are you fucking serious right now?" His voice had lost some of that silky-smooth quality, frustration and weariness creating ripples. But he shuffled forward.

"Follow my voice." I reached a hand out. It was so dark I may as well have had my eyes closed. If I hadn't been half-convinced we were about to break up (were we even together?) it would've been fun, seeking each other out in the dark.

My hand bumped his chest . . . and stayed there.

"There you are." He lowered his voice, his hand landing on my ribs, then shifting up to my shoulder.

I felt so distant from him, so uncertain of who he was, what *we* were. But I couldn't stop myself from getting closer. My feet shuffled forward; my other hand settled on his hip. And then we were moving as one, stepping into each other's space, hands tentative at first but incapable of holding back. My arms wrapped around his waist, and his banded around my back. We were chest to chest. With my cheek over his heart, I listened to the *thud-thud* as my breathing began to match his without my even realizing it.

For a few moments, we just stood there, holding each other. I felt at home in his arms, even though I'd touched him only a handful of times through the bamboo and kissed him only once.

His soft voice broke the silence. "Mena, what are we doing here?"

"It's called hugging." He'd torn through my defenses without much more than his touch and solid presence. My mind had calmed, the churning in my stomach had settled, and I'd reverted to our usual banter. But there was nothing normal about this situation—about me.

"I'd like to turn on the light."

"No. Please, Turner, don't." I tried to pull away, fully prepared to find an exit and run before he could see me. But he held on. His grip was firm but not insistent. I could've wrenched out of it if I'd really wanted to. I didn't want to.

His chest expanded against mine in a deep sigh, which turned into a soft growl at the end. "I don't understand this. We've been getting to know each other for weeks. I've told you things . . . I don't care what you look like, Mena. I like you—your mind, your sense of humor, how you feel in my arms. What is the big deal? Why won't you tell me who you are?"

I smiled sadly at how direct he was being. It was incredible to know he felt this connection between us just as strongly as I did.

But he'd been hanging out with Jayden and his friends more and more. I'd seen Steph and Bonnie hovering around him, giving him flirty looks. He was falling into the worst possible group, and I wasn't sure if it was too late.

"I'm sorry, Turner. I know this is frustrating for you. But once you find out who I am . . . it'll change everything."

"No." He squeezed me. "It'll change nothing. At least not for me. Are you really that insecure about your looks?"

"Yes. No. Argh!" This time I did push out of his embrace. My hands dropped to his waist, my body unwilling to separate from him completely, but I needed some space to breathe. He smelled so damn good; I wanted to give him whatever he wanted so I could continue to bury my nose in his chest and breathe in that warm fresh-rain scent. "It's not just about that. There are things you don't know. About me. About this school. I . . ."

"So tell me. Why can't you just be honest? Haven't I earned your trust?"

And just like that, I remembered why I'd been questioning everything in the first place.

"Don't act like I'm the only one keeping secrets, Turner. You can't demand honesty if you're not willing to give it."

"What's that supposed to mean?" His voice rose a little in pitch. He was getting frustrated. So was I.

My heart rate quickened, and before I could chicken out, I blurted, "I saw you yesterday. Talking to Jayden's little sister."

His muscles tensed under my fingers. He went very still, his thumbs no longer rubbing little absent-minded circles against my shoulders.

"How much did you hear?" The ocean-smooth quality that made me want to sink into his voice was gone—this smoothness was like glass. Sharp and deadly.

What the fuck had I been thinking locking myself in a dark place with a guy I suspected was ... doing *something* to sweet, innocent little Jenny? I was a fucking moron.

"Nothing. I hardly heard a word, and I only saw you guys talking for, like, two minutes." I removed my hands from his sides and took a step back, mentally calculating if I was closer to the door that led to the gym or the one that led outside.

"Shit." He sighed, and his hands found my hips. "You sound fucking terrified. I'm sorry. Please ... I didn't mean to be so intense. I just ... I don't know what to say."

He sounded genuine, but he hadn't answered my unasked question. What the fuck was he doing with Jenny? I put my hands on his arms, ready to push him off if I had to, fighting the urge to pull him closer.

"What was that about then?" I asked. "I didn't hear much, but that girl looked fucking terrified."

"I know. I didn't put that look on her face. Trust me."

"Never trust someone who says *trust me*."

He chuckled, and it turned into a groan. "I can't really tell you much more about that situation—the secrets are not ... it's not just my story to tell. But I'm trying to do something good. I'm trying to do the right thing."

"Is she in some kind of trouble?" My nails dug into his forearms. She'd defended him when I confronted her. Was it possible the fear in her eyes wasn't *of* him but *for* him?

"Maybe. I promise I'll tell you the full story when it's all over. And I hope that will be sooner rather than later. In the meantime, I have to ask you to trust me. Trust that I'm doing the right thing."

My gut was telling me I could. The idea of Turner doing something malicious was so discordant with the guy I'd gotten to know. It just didn't fit.

And Jenny had defended him.

He hadn't threatened me or even raised his voice. He hadn't demanded I keep my mouth shut. He was just asking me to trust him.

I decided to take a leap of faith and do just that.

"OK, I'll trust you, but I'll be keeping an eye on Jenny."

He released a heavy breath. "That would be amazing, actually. I can't be around twenty-four seven, and knowing she has another person I trust in her corner actually makes me feel a lot better."

I dragged my hands up his arms to rest on his shoulders. "But you have to trust me too. I know it's frustrating for you, but I need you to trust that my reasons for keeping my identity secret are not frivolous. I just need time. I've been my true self with you in every other way, I promise."

"I believe you. I'll try to be patient." He pulled me flush against his chest and kissed me on the forehead, his lips landing off-center, as he couldn't see me.

But I could *feel* him. Every hard muscle pressing against me. His strong arms holding me, making me feel safe, even after I'd felt scared just moments ago.

"Did we just have our first fight?" His shoulders shook under my hands with quiet laughter.

"I dunno." I shrugged. "Aren't fights something couples have?"

"Is that not what we are?"

"Oh . . . uh . . . you're not seeing anyone else?"

"You are?" He suddenly sounded a little worried, a little unsure. "I mean, I'm not interested in anyone else."

"Good. Neither am I." Not that I had any other options. He was it for me, and I wouldn't change that for the world. But he had girls all over school hanging off him. There was no question he'd been asked out several times already. Had he said yes to any of them?

"Good." A smile warmed his voice, and his hands started rubbing small circles on my lower back.

"Are you sure about this? You don't know what I look like." I couldn't help feeling a bit insecure.

"I'm not falling for your looks, Mena. I'm falling for your personality. And this fine body." He gave me a squeeze on the hips, his strong fingers only just digging into the area above my ass.

I laughed and dropped my forehead to his shoulder.

"Now, since we've survived our first fight"—his low words reverberated through my chest—"we really should make up."

"Oh?" I smiled into his shirt, then tilted my head to speak just beneath his jaw. "And how do you propose we do that?"

I punctuated my suggestive question with a soft, lingering kiss to the side of his neck.

His voice was as breathy as mine when he answered. "I have a few ideas."

CHAPTER 8

I KISSED HIM AGAIN, A LITTLE HIGHER, GETTING drunk on how his arms tightened around me every time my lips connected, how his breathing grew shallower. Emboldened by his reaction, I did something I'd been daydreaming about since I got a good look at him—I darted my tongue out and licked his jaw. Just a little lick right under his ear.

He exhaled sharply and turned his head, his lips searching for mine in the dark. I tipped my face up and met him halfway.

We kissed as if we were reuniting lovers, back together after being unsure we'd ever see the other again—tongues tangling, hands tugging at clothing. The bell rang as we started to back toward the rear wall of the room, neither of us willing to break the kiss. My back connected with the stack of gym mats, and Turner smacked one hand beside my head for balance as he leaned his body flush against mine.

He pulled his delicious lips away and croaked

against my burning cheek, "We should get to class."

"Fuck that." I managed to get my hands between us and pulled the zipper of his hoodie down, stroking his chest and hard abs all the way down to the waistband of his jeans. He groaned as my hands slid under his T-shirt, my thumbs rubbing those hipbones I'd been at eye level with in the library.

Just like that day, I had the urge to kneel down and lick them, but I settled for copping a good feel. I'd never given anyone a blow job—I wasn't sure I was ready for that—and getting on my knees and licking that general area was sure to lead to a dick in my mouth.

Instead, my hands ghosted up his back, drawing him against me. The discordant thud of basketballs on polished wood only just registered—a gym class was starting. I vaguely hoped they wouldn't need any other equipment.

Turner kissed me deeply, in smooth, rhythmic strokes of his tongue against mine. His hand went to the back of my head and, finding my hair up in a ponytail, gripped the hair tie firmly and tugged. It stung for a second, and then my hair tumbled down around us.

He inhaled deeply and broke the kiss to whisper against my lips, "You smell so good. Like strawberries."

My response was an incoherent moan. I was beyond words, completely lost in the lust; the heavy, heady feeling low in my belly; the ache between my legs.

I rolled my hips against his, and his body responded, his hips meeting mine in a steady rhythm.

"You *feel* fucking good too," he growled.

I forcefully pushed my lips once more against his. I could drown in his voice, find bliss in the gritty quality I'd put there. But I needed his lips on mine.

I widened my legs, bent my left knee. He took it in his big hand and hooked it over his hip.

And then I could feel him, his hardness right there, giving me exactly the friction I was craving.

I moaned loudly. Too loudly.

The sound bounced off the walls, reminding me where we were. My sudden rush of adrenaline only added to the heady cocktail of pleasure already coursing through my veins.

Turner started kissing and licking my jaw, his mouth moving down toward my neck as his hand traveled up my front. He caressed my breast over the fabric of my T-shirt, his hand almost completely covering it, while our hips kept up a steady rhythm.

Then he was pushing up under my T-shirt, pushing my bra out of the way so he could fondle me skin-to-skin.

He groaned into my mouth, the sound going straight to my core. Maybe I was ready for a blow job after all—I wanted to hear him make that sound over and over. I wanted to be the one to wrench it from his throat. I wanted all our clothing gone. I wanted a bed instead of the stinky old gym mats at my back.

Something banged against the door, making us both jump.

We stopped kissing and froze, only our hips still rocking slightly as we panted and listened, suddenly thrown back into reality.

"I said *no* contact, Andrews! How in the hell did you two end up there?" The coach sounded mad but a little amused.

The class's chorus of laughter followed, along with a loud male guffaw right on the other side of the door. The door that stood between an entire class of sophomores and Turner and me.

"Shit." I pushed gently against his chest, and he removed his hand from my breast. I missed it already. I never wanted to wear a bra again—Turner could just walk behind me, holding my boobs in place with his big, warm hands, all day every day.

"Since you're there, grab the orange cones, would ya?" The coach shouted again.

"Fuck." This time it was Turner's turn to curse.

I adjusted my bra and ran a hand through my hair. Snatching up my bag, I rushed in the general direction of the football-field door and ended up walking right into it, bumping my knee with a grunt.

"Mena?" Turner hissed into the dark. "Fuck, what are we gonna do?"

"I'm sorry. I gotta go. Just hide or something."

"What?" He sounded panicked, but I was running on pure adrenaline now. I had to get out of there *immediately*.

I found the door handle just as the other door creaked open. Thankfully, mine opened inward, blocking me from view as light flooded the room.

I closed the door behind me and threw my hood up, thanking every deity imaginable that no one was on the football field as I powerwalked away. I'd go to the bathroom to get my shit together and kill more time before my next class started.

No one—not even Turner—stopped me as I hurried off, and I smiled, my chest heaving. I couldn't believe we'd gotten away with it. I just hoped Turner hadn't been busted.

* * *

"Not too dark on the eyes, Philly. I want to look sophisticated, not slutty," my mom directed me as I started applying eyeshadow to her lids.

"Eew! Why the hell would I make my mother look slutty?"

We'd set up at the kitchen table, all my makeup spread out, Mom at my mercy. She'd come home in almost as good a mood as me—declared we'd get Chinese for dinner, but it would be just me and Dad, as she was going to a seminar thing, and could I please do her makeup?

I took pretty much any excuse to do makeup, so there we were.

She smiled. "I didn't mean you'd do it on purpose, sweetheart."

"So, you just think I'm shit at makeup," I deadpanned.

"What?" She backed away from my brush and opened her eyes. "No, Philomena, I was just trying to crack a joke."

I snorted and let my grin burst through. "I know. I'm just messing with you, Mom."

She breathed a massive sigh of relief and closed her eyes again so I could get back to work. "I just don't know these days. And please don't take this the wrong way, but you get in your moods, and I . . . well, I worry about you sometimes."

I paused for a second and looked into my mom's face, her eyes closed, her chin tipped up. We looked so similar, but her eyes were a little more tired, her lips marred with a few lines. She was still pretty. It didn't make sense, because I *wasn't* pretty. How the hell did that work?

I got back to work, fighting the urge to tell her everything. The messages, the taunts, the way I was ignored at school, even the few incidents where I'd actually been attacked.

But then I swallowed around the lump in my throat and shoved down that urge. There was literally nothing she could do. No point in adding further stress to my parents' already frantic lives.

"Anyway, you're in a good mood today." Mom broke the silence before I could. "It's nice to see."

"Yeah I . . . had a good day." I couldn't stop the smile pulling at my lips as I thought about what Turner and I had been doing in the storage room just hours earlier.

Mom cracked one eye open and gave me a sly grin. "I know that smile."

"You know nothing, woman. Close your eyes." I gave her a very serious look, but the smile broke out again as soon as her eye closed.

"You have a crush," Mom sing-songed.

"Mom." I laughed, then after a pause, added, "It's more than a crush."

What the hell had just possessed me to imply to my mother I was seeing a boy? Maybe I was just desperate to tell someone, bursting with the excitement Turner made me feel.

"Holy shit, my Sweet Chilly Philly has a boyfriend!" My mother squealed like a preteen and backed out of the reach of my makeup brush.

"Mother." I shot her a withering look.

"OK, OK, I'll try to have more chill," she said while bouncing in her chair.

I rolled my eyes. "I can't finish your makeup if you're bouncing around like that."

She stopped and closed her eyes again, tipping her face up. I sighed and got back to work.

After a few minutes she asked, "What's his name?"

"Uh . . . I . . ."

"Don't tell me you don't know his name." She chuckled.

"Of course I know his name." *He just doesn't know mine.* "I'm just . . . it's kind of new."

"OK, I respect your privacy. I just have to ask, Philomena, do we need to have the safe-sex talk?"

"Mom!" Now it was my turn to screech. "No. I am well across safe sex, and we do *not* need to discuss this."

"Fine." Her expression grew suddenly serious. "Just promise you'll come to me if you need to, OK? I'll never judge you or be mad if you need help."

The urge to tell her about how miserable high school was nearly overwhelmed me again. "I know. Thanks, Mom."

She smiled and nodded. "And for the love of god, don't get pregnant."

"Jesus fuc . . ." I put the brush away, done with her eyes. "Look down so I can do your mascara."

She obeyed, and I changed the topic immediately. "So, what exactly is this thing you're going to? Chelsea from work has mentioned going to the same thing, and it sounds a little new-agey to me."

"Oh, yes, I think I met Chelsea at the first info session I went to a few weeks ago. She's lovely. And Boyd Burrows runs the sessions. He's Jayden's dad—you two go to school together, right?"

"Ugh. Unfortunately."

"Oh, you're not friends?"

"Not exactly. How's that?" I held a mirror in front of her, blocking my own scowl at the mention of Jayden. I wanted to ask if Chelsea and Boyd seemed close at the last session—I was curious if that was the reason behind Chelsea's sudden enthusiasm for these seminars—but Mom would only lecture me about not gossiping, so I kept my mouth shut.

"I look ten years younger! This is amazing! Thank you."

"You're welcome." I gave her a genuine smile. I really hadn't done much—covered up the dark circles, accentuated her eyes. "You didn't answer my question about this event," I said as I started to pack up, separating the brushes that needed to be cleaned.

"Oh, it's nothing 'new-agey,' as you put it. BestLyf is a large, successful professional-development company. They have offices all over the country and run workshops and courses. That kind of thing. It's all about improving yourself while improving your skills. It's hard to explain unless you come along and experience it for yourself. It's very motivating."

"I can see that. There's not much that will get you out of the house on a school night."

"It's worth it. But I'm not sure it's going to keep happening. I've got another two events that they offer free of charge, then the next level up is paid workshops and retreats, and I just don't think we can afford it." She sighed.

There wasn't much I could say to that. Whether it was my mother wanting to improve her skills, my father wanting to spend time with his friends on a fishing trip, or me wanting to get away from my abusers—*we couldn't afford it.*

"I hope you and Dad find the money for it, Mom. I like seeing you happy and motivated."

"Thanks, sweetheart, but you don't need to worry about that." She waved her hand dismissively as she walked off toward the kitchen. "How about a snack?"

"Sure."

We spent the next half hour munching on celery sticks slathered in peanut butter. Mom managed to bring the conversation back to boys and started reminiscing about all the "shenanigans" she and Auntie Em had gotten up to when they were my age and running amok all over Devilbend.

Thankfully, Dad came home and saved me from hearing anything that would have scarred me for life, and Mom left for her meeting.

Turner wasn't home that evening, but whatever he was up to with his dad, he had time to text me occasionally.

> **T:** I can't believe you managed to slip away without me seeing you! I'm once again convinced you work for the CIA.

> **M:** How many times do I have to tell you—it's the FBI.

> **T:** Maybe it's the KGB. They use beautiful women to lure men with their wiles.

> **M:** Wiles? LOL!

> **T:** Yes. You have incredible wiles. I'm still hard just thinking about your wiles.

I looked over my shoulder to make sure my dad was nowhere around. He was glued to the TV on the other side of the balcony door, but I still dropped my hands low in my lap before replying.

> **M:** We definitely have some unfinished business. I can't stop thinking about it either.

> **T:** If my dad wasn't sitting right next to me, I'd be describing all the things I want to do to you next time.

> **M:** Change of topic then! Did you get into trouble?

> **T:** Nah. Luckily the kid who came into the room as you ran away was someone I know— he's on the football team. He gave me shit about having a girl in there and tried to get me to say who it was, but he covered for me with the coach, and I slipped out the back door.

> **M:** Good. I was worried you might get caught.

> **T:** But not worried enough to hang around.

> **M:** I'm sorry! I panicked!

T: It's OK. I'm teasing!

I went to bed with a smile on my face.

But life's a bitch, so anything good that happened to me naturally had to be balanced out by something shitty.

CHAPTER 9

MADISON MUST'VE BEEN IN A BAD MOOD, because she seemed to have made it her mission to make my life hell all day.

She bumped into me from behind on my way to first period, making me drop my books, then declared, "You dropped something" in a monotone before walking away, as if I were gum on the bottom of her shoe.

Between second and third period, I was at my locker when the whole group walked past. Bonnie slammed my locker door on my arm, and when I wrenched back, wincing, Kelsey slammed the door shut.

"How careless, leaving a locker wide open like that." Madison was already walking away, the other girls snickering.

I rubbed my arm and flexed my fingers. That was going to leave a bruise.

At lunch, I made the mistake of walking past the cafeteria on my way to hide out in the library.

Jayden rounded the corner just as I passed the

doors, his arm slung over Madison's shoulders, their friends trailing behind them. Turner was with them.

My heart skipped a beat—I wasn't sure if it was from seeing him or from fear. I hunched my shoulders and tried to slip past, hugging the wall, but it was too late.

"What is that *smell*?" Jayden waved his hand in front of his face exaggeratedly.

Madison gave me a satisfied, cruel smirk as the others blocked my path. Turner paused halfway through the cafeteria doors and turned around with a frown.

"I hope that's not coming from the cafeteria. I swear, the standards at this school are slipping." Steph tutted. Everyone laughed.

I wanted the floor to open up and swallow me, anything to keep Turner from seeing this. Hopefully they'd get bored or hungry quickly.

"I mean, everything looks clean, but . . ." Steph looked around, making it obvious I was invisible in this scenario—like a bad smell.

"What's that stuff? That gas that comes off volcanoes?" Jayden snapped his fingers. "Smells like rotten eggs. It's in fertilizer and shit."

"Sulphur," Turner supplied, his voice flat, emotionless.

It wasn't until that moment that I realized I'd been hoping he would say something, *do* something, to stop them. No, he didn't know I was Mena—the girl he'd been talking to all this time. But I hadn't thought he was the kind of person to be OK with assholes being assholes for no reason.

My heart cracked in my chest; I couldn't make myself look at him. I couldn't make myself look at any of them as they continued to pretend I didn't exist while cracking jokes about how bad I smelled.

I blocked out the rest of their words, keeping my head down as my eyes searched for a way out.

"We gonna stand out here all lunch? I'm fucking starving." Turner's deep voice was the only thing that could've made me tune back in. My head unconsciously turned in his direction, but years of habit kept my eyes low.

His right hand was in a fist by his side; his other arm lifted and flopped back down in a frustrated gesture. A small blue band circled his wrist—a hair tie. *My* hair tie.

As shitty as it felt to be standing there copping their shit, a tiny flare of warmth erupted in my chest.

They all followed Turner into the cafeteria without another glance at me, and I rushed away, gulping air, suddenly realizing how hard it had been to breathe just moments before.

After that, I was extra vigilant to avoid them and made it to my last class without another incident.

Moments after I arrived, Turner wandered in and sat in the seat directly in front of me—the seat he'd occupied since school started. It had gotten increasingly more difficult not to reach out and touch him, brush a bit of lint off his collar, run my hands through his soft, messy hair. But I restrained myself, not even looking at him too much.

Jayden sat next to him, and I tried just as hard to

ignore him too, albeit for vastly different reasons.

The first half of the class was spent discussing *The Crucible*, the second half working on an upcoming assignment. Most of the students fell into silence, hunched over their books, as Mr. Chen buried his face in his laptop and typed away furiously.

It wasn't long before people lost focus, and several surreptitiously pulled out their phones. After a long and stressful day, my concentration was lacking too. The words on the page kept blurring; I'd read the same sentence three times, and it still wouldn't register in my brain. I kept finding myself glancing around the room, forcing my gaze away from Turner's broad shoulders hunched over his desk, the short hair at the nape of his neck, the way his knee was bouncing lightly. I knew how hard those shoulders were, what that hair felt like under my palm, what a thrill it had been when that knee pushed its way between my legs.

I bit my lip to keep from smiling and shifted in my seat, pointing my eyes back down at my book. After a few moments, I looked around the room again. No one was paying me a lick of attention, so I chanced another ogling of my boyfriend (I couldn't believe I had a secret boyfriend!).

Turner shifted, extending the leg that had been bouncing a moment earlier. He leaned his head on his left hand, totally slouched in the desk that looked tiny supporting his big frame. His right hand hung off the edge of the desk, and his fingers were fiddling with something.

Those fingers . . . the things those fingers had made me feel, the places on my body they had touched, the places I still wanted them to explore . . .

My inappropriate fantasizing evaporated when I noticed he had my hair tie in his nimble fingers, twisting it around his pointer finger, stretching it out, scrunching it up. I'd tried not to read too much into the fact that he'd kept it, but I couldn't help wondering.

I glanced around the class again. At least half of them had their phones out now, and several people were chatting at their desks, abandoning any semblance of doing work. I ached to take my own phone out and text my boyfriend, but that was dangerous. What if someone read over my shoulder? What if someone took it or broke it or both? What if they started teasing me about why I even had a phone when I had no one to message?

The anxiety almost overwhelmed me, but it also pissed me off. I didn't want my life to be dictated by bullies. It wasn't fucking fair.

I didn't want to be Phil—the sad, friendless loser everyone picked on. I wanted to be Mena—the normal teenage girl who had a boyfriend she could secretly text in class. So, I pulled my phone out, hiding it behind the bulk of my textbook, and surreptitiously did just that.

M: You have something of mine.

I kept my head down, pretending to read, as I watched him in my periphery. He pulled his phone out and read the text under the desk, sitting up a little straighter.

Would he deny it? Would he be confused? Maybe he didn't put as much meaning into it as I had.

My phone flashed with his reply.

> **T:** You left it when you ran away from me. I'm holding on to it, as per the finders-keepers rules. You can't have it!

> **M:** LOL! OK. Why so intense about a little hair tie?

He chuckled, glancing at the teacher before lifting his phone onto his desk. He tapped away at the screen, but my phone didn't go off. I frowned. Maybe he was texting someone else.

He shook his head lightly and tapped some more. Then he grunted and ran his hand through his messy hair before tapping at the phone a third time.

I was wondering who was making him frustrated when my phone finally went off again.

> **T:** I like having something of yours with me since you already have something of mine.

I racked my brain but couldn't think of a single item of his I'd even held, so I replied with several question marks.

His reply was instant.

T: My heart.

My breath hitched. My eyes stayed glued to my little screen, my body frozen. He felt it as deeply as I did—this connection between us. I could hardly believe it.

In front of me, Turner shifted in his seat and blew out a big breath. He wiped both hands down the fronts of his thighs, his head bent over his screen.

I tried to think of the perfect response. Something simple and heartfelt that wouldn't come off gushy but would show him how hard I was falling for him.

Before I could find the words, another text came in.

T: Too much?

I smiled and suddenly found it easier to reply. His nervousness was putting me at ease.

M: Not too much. You have mine too.

I added a heart emoji and sent it.

He leaned back in his chair and laced his fingers behind his head, giving me a good view of his defined arms, as he sighed—the relief palpable.

"You good, man?" Jayden asked next to him, breaking my happy bubble. The soft murmurings of the class came back into focus, and I remembered where I was—shark-infested water. I couldn't show any of these people the gaping hole in my chest where my heart thudded for the boy sitting in front of me. They could smell blood in the water, and my heart was overflowing.

I tucked my phone back into my bag.

"Yeah. I'm fucking perfect." I could hear the smile in Turner's voice, and apparently, Jayden could see it.

"That is the most goofy-ass smile I've ever seen, bro. You got a chick on the hook?" Jayden nudged Turner's shoulder, and my boyfriend laughed, neither denying nor confirming Jayden's suspicion.

"Holy shit, you do!" Jayden announced a little too loudly, his exclamation masked by the bell. "Who is it? Is it Kelsey? She's been all up in your crotch since the first day of school. Is it Bonnie? She gives it up to everyone though, man. Be careful of her. Oh, wait! Is it Steph?"

We all packed up and got to our feet, eager to get home.

I waited until Turner and Jayden were making their way out, carefully staying out of their line of sight. Not even Jayden could completely ruin the buzz of Turner's adorable semi-declaration of love.

Even so, it still stung that by the time we'd made it out into the hall, Jayden had named almost every single girl in our year and even a few juniors, and my name wasn't even mentioned as a joke.

CHAPTER 10

FOR TWO GLORIOUS WEEKS, TURNER AND I flirted unashamedly via text, sending each other messages I would have been horrified for anyone else to read. We met up in the storage area off the gym a few more times, but we had to be careful not to get caught. And I had to be careful not to let him see me.

Friday after school, it was pouring down rain but still kind of warm, in a humid way. Naturally, I didn't have an umbrella with me, so I got drenched on my walk home. After a shower, I planted myself on the balcony, resigned to the fact that my hair was going to frizz up.

Rain continued to pelt down, the afternoon sky prematurely dark due to the heavy clouds.

I thought about doing a makeup look, but that just made me feel guilty; I had a World History assignment, Statistics homework, and the assignment on *The Crucible* to work on. Plus, the weather was too humid, and the light outside was too crap. I was hoping Turner might come out to his balcony later.

I slumped in the chair, propped my feet up on the little table, and pulled my phone out. I should've been dragging my books out and starting on my homework if I was going to be tragically pining for my boyfriend on the balcony. *Oh god!* I was basically Juliet. Did that mean this love story was doomed to end in tragedy?

Apparently, I was a massive procrastinator as well as a Juliet, because I pushed all thoughts of homework out of my mind and started scrolling Instagram. I did my best to get lost in the makeup pics and cute dog videos, but ignoring the DNHS Confessions posts was almost impossible. Every time the distinctive burgundy (our school color) background popped up, a jolt of anxiety shot up my spine. I scrolled past as fast as possible, but when I started seeing Turner's name crop up, I couldn't help myself. I went onto the page and looked.

There were the usual posts about how ugly my birthmark—and pretty much everything else about me— was and how I should just put myself out of my misery. But speculation about who Turner was sneaking off to see had finally reached the wide gossip network. It was inevitable that someone would notice eventually.

One post, dated three days ago, read, "Caught a glimpse of Turner making out with someone with shiny blonde hair behind the science building at lunch. Bonnie was also mysteriously not at lunch." It made me gag, but I knew it was a flat-out lie, because I'd been pushing Turner against the gym mats in the storage room at lunch three days ago. Bonnie had probably sent it in herself.

There were several other posts in the same vein, including a few pics of the girls that had made my life hell leaning into him, whispering in his ear, touching his shoulder. I wanted to throw my phone off the balcony so I would never have to see that shit again.

"Fucking bitches," I growled, squeezing the device in my hand.

"Hey, neighbor." Turner's voice sounded a bit wary. "You OK?"

Shit. I'd been so absorbed by the bullshit on social media that I hadn't even heard him come out. "Hey, stranger. Yeah, I'm fine. Just crap on Instagram."

There was a beat of silence, the relentless rain humming all around us.

"You know none of that shit is true, right?" His ocean-calm voice was serious. "I'd tell them all I was yours if you'd let me."

You wouldn't want to be mine if you knew who I really was. The thought flew through my mind before I could stop it, surprising me a little with its intensity. My chest suddenly felt tight.

I wanted so badly to show him who I really was.

I wanted to show them all the truth.

I wanted to run away and never see any of them again.

Before I had a chance to answer, the sound of Turner's balcony door sliding open cut through the sound of the rain.

"Turner?" It was his dad.

"Hey, Dad. You're home early." Turner shifted; I

could just make out the outline of his body as he got to his feet.

"Work was quiet. What are you doing out here? It's pouring. Never mind. How was today? Did you speak to her? Did you convince her?"

I kept still, frowning in confusion. Was he talking about me? Had Turner confided in his dad? I couldn't really be mad about that, but it didn't make sense. His dad sounded really intense about it.

"No, Dad. I would've messaged you right away. Let's talk inside."

Whatever it was, Turner clearly didn't want me to know. I wasn't the only one keeping secrets.

I tried not to let it get to me, but it was hard not to feel hurt when I was already in a vulnerable, self-conscious state. My feet fell to the floor, and I leaned my elbows on my knees and dropped my head in my hands. What the fuck was I doing? This needed to stop. I had to tell him the truth—the whole awful history. If he decided he didn't want me after, then I didn't want him either. The thought of losing him—not just losing him but being *rejected* by him—felt like a punch to the gut, and tears welled in my eyes.

My phone went off, and I reached for the welcome distraction.

It was my boss.

> **Leah:** Hey, Philly. Are you free to work the dinner shift tomorrow night? Chelsea canceled on me again.

M: Again? Sure, I'll be there.

Chelsea had bailed on three shifts in the last two weeks, and I was starting to worry for her job. Leah was not happy.

L: Thanks, lovely. You're a lifesaver!

I headed inside to start on my homework, telling myself I needed the money and that taking the shift had nothing to do with wanting to delay my chat with Turner.

Saturday nights were always busy at work. Tonight there were three other waitresses on with me, two cooks in the back, and Leah floating around helping where she could, constantly cursing Chelsea's name under her breath for bailing on us.

About halfway through the dinner rush, Donna, Harlow, and Amaya came in with a group of their friends from school. I wasn't sure what they were doing on the shitty side of town, and I didn't have time to ask them; I just greeted them all warmly and seated them in a booth in my section before rushing off.

The girls had seen my birthmark plenty of times, of course, but most of their friends saw me only occasionally at parties and things. Thankfully, none of them seemed to care about it, although I did notice Nicola lean over the table and whisper to Donna, who gave her a withering look and then waved her hand dismissively. I couldn't help but wonder if they were talking about me.

I seated a couple and cleared another table before going back to take their order.

"What can I get you guys?"

"What's good?" William asked. Will had neat brown hair and had been on again/off again with Donna for nearly a year.

"Uh, the loaded nachos are pretty good, and we have a great pecan pie—it's the owner's nana's recipe."

"Hey, Mena." Drew, a guy with black hair who drove a car probably worth more than our apartment, flashed me a grin. We'd hooked up once at a party. He was nice enough, but we really didn't have anything in common. "I'll have the nachos, but when can I take you out?"

"Oh my god." I rolled my eyes but laughed lightly. He'd asked me out a few times, always in front of other people. I suspected he was doing it more to show off than because he actually wanted to date me.

"Leave her alone, Drew." Harlow slapped his shoulder. "Mena's spoken for."

"What? No." He groaned, a little over the top.

"Yeah, it's true love. You can't compete," Donna added.

"Not that she'll give us any damn details on the guy." Amaya glanced up from her phone long enough to give me a reproachful look.

"Stop," I hissed at them but struggled to keep the smile off my face. Any mention of Turner had me feeling giddy. "Are you assholes going to order or what? I'm kind of fucking busy."

"Two servings of nachos." Drew pouted. "I need to eat my feelings tonight."

I rolled my eyes at him and took the other orders.

I was elated no one had made a big deal about my birthmark, and being around the girls always made me feel good. Maybe I could even sit with them on my break—if it ever slowed down enough for me to take a break.

As I headed for the servery to place their order with the kitchen, the door swung open, the little old-fashioned bell dinging. My smile fell, a heavy weight dropping in the pit of my churning stomach.

Jayden swaggered through the door as though he owned the place, his hand clasped around Madison's. I caught a glimpse of the rest of their group before dropping my gaze and rushing behind the counter.

After placing the order, I caught one of the other waitresses as she passed. "I'm running to the bathroom," I told her, then hurried to the back before she could answer.

In the dingy toilet, I took a few deep breaths to try to slow my racing heart. With a conscious effort, I pulled the impassive mask I wore at school over my features and hoped they'd eat quickly and get the fuck out before they noticed me.

I couldn't leave the other waitresses in the middle of the dinner rush for long, so I forced myself back just in time to see Leah handing my worst enemies menus. She'd seated them in the booth directly next to Donna and her crew—in my section.

I groaned internally as dread settled around me like a heavy mist, making it hard to breathe or move or think straight. I cleared another table, kind of hoping one of the other girls would take their order—we weren't super strict on sections. But we were slammed, and I had no luck.

Having done all I could to avoid it, I sighed and dragged my feet over to their booth. My shoulders slumped, my chest caving in on itself farther with every step I took. When I reached their table, I took the pen and pad out of my apron pocket and cleared my throat, glancing up.

The flat, professional "*Can I take your order?*" died in my throat.

Seated between Bonnie and Kelsey, his elbows casually on the table, was Turner.

Fuck, he was beautiful, with his bomber jacket and his already dark eyes obscured further by the shadow of a baseball cap. He was grinning, his strong shoulders shaking lightly at something Jayden was saying across the table.

But I didn't have time to dwell on that. A full-blown tempest of panic, horror, and crippling uncertainty was writhing inside me. What the hell was I supposed to do now? I couldn't let him find out like this.

I looked around at all of them, hoping like hell I didn't seem like a deer in headlights, even though I felt like one. No one was looking at me. Maybe it had finally happened. Maybe all their jokes about me being invisible had finally translated into reality. I could only hope.

Turner noticed me standing there like a mute idiot.

"Oh, hey, sorry." He gave me a quick glance and a little smile. "I'll have the cheeseburger. Extra fries."

I responded with a tight, polite smile and jotted his order down as the others all groaned, a couple of them throwing napkins at him.

"What?" He looked confused but laughed as he defended himself from the onslaught.

"Didn't you see we were all waiting to see how long she'd stand there, not saying anything like a weirdo?" Steph filled him in.

"Uh . . . no." Turner shifted in his seat and flashed me a wary look.

I just stood there, humiliated, hoping against hope they'd just order and I could slink away without saying something.

I'd talk to Turner after work. I'd tell him everything. I couldn't keep doing this.

After an extended silence—my eyes glued to the table, my fingers gripping the pen so tightly my fingers were beginning to hurt—Turner cleared his throat.

"I'm starving. Fucking order already." He said it with a smile in his voice, but I heard the growly tension underneath.

Another beat of silence, and then Madison made a show of studying the menu, tapping one manicured finger against her chin. The others snickered.

This was taking way too long. I had two other tables waiting to order; all the other staff were rushing around like crazy. But walking away, trying to ignore them as they did me, would only make it worse.

"Is the chicken pie homemade?" Kelsey asked.

I pressed my lips together and nodded.

"What about the pasta? Is that gluten free?" Steph asked.

It took physical effort not to grind my teeth or roll my eyes. I shook my head no.

Then Madison put the nail in my coffin. "I'd like to hear the specials."

She leaned back in her seat and crossed her arms, giving me a smug look.

I hated her in that moment. I'd hated her so many times over the last few years, but in *that moment*, my hatred for her was seething and pure. She was taking my choice away. She was forcing me to expose myself to Turner in front of all of them, at work, with my only friends in the world *right there*. Donna's table had gone silent. I could feel their eyes on me, but I could focus on only one crisis at a time. I couldn't imagine what they were thinking. I was *so* humiliated.

And the worst thing was—Madison didn't even know any of these things. She just had a natural instinct for making my life hell.

With no other options, I pulled my shoulders back. I refused to do this while cowering, even though every survival instinct I had was urging me to hunch over and duck my head, scurry away like a mouse from a cat. I hoped it looked casual as I told them about the specials, my voice clear and steady—even though I was dying on the inside.

I looked directly at them as I spoke, but I didn't see them. My full focus was on Turner.

He'd been fiddling with the corner of a napkin when Madison had asked for the specials, his face turned down, one arm slung over the back of the booth behind Bonnie's shoulders. When I started to speak, he froze. Every muscle in his body seemed to tense. His jaw twitched; his long fingers wrapped around the napkin and squeezed.

He knew. How could he not?

But why wasn't he looking at me? Was he repulsed now that he knew who I was?

I couldn't stand this. I needed to be away from this whole mess. I let some frustration leak into my voice. "We're really busy tonight. What's your order?"

Several cutting looks were thrown in my direction.

"Don't rush me," Kelsey snapped.

Tears pricked the backs of my eyes. I was done. I'd send one of the other girls to deal with them.

Before I could book it out of there, Turner spoke. "Hey, neighbor," he said in that ocean-calm way, his eyes still downcast and hidden by the hat, not looking at me.

He wanted to confirm it was really me, but he didn't want any of them to know. Was he protecting me? Or himself? I so badly wanted to give him the benefit of the doubt. I'd been adamant I didn't want anyone to know about us. Maybe now he understood the implications. Maybe he was honoring my wishes.

But he'd still just sat there as they treated me like shit. This moment had been taken from me—just as they took everything else.

White-hot anger crawled up my spine, giving me the strength to remain upright.

"Oh, shit." Jayden laughed. "You two are neighbors? That fucking sucks, bro. Imagine having to look at that face even when at home."

A muscle in Turner's jaw ticked. Someone slammed something onto the table at Donna's booth. *Please, god, don't come over here.*

"You must be confused. You've never seen me . . . stranger." I hoped he got my meaning. He'd never seen me *really*—not this ugly, twisted, ground-into-the dirt side of me. Not like this.

The heat at my spine was going to my head, the rage turning to frustration and despair as the backs of my eyes started to sting. I really fucking didn't want to cry in front of everyone.

Turner rested both elbows on the surface of the table and twisted his head to look at me. I dropped my eyes before they could meet his. I didn't want him looking at me. I wanted to crawl into a hole and *die*.

"I'll have the cob salad." Madison placed the menu on the table delicately, as if we'd all been waiting for her to make up her mind. As if I wasn't standing there completely destroyed inside. Was she that oblivious? Or was she turning the knife?

The others followed her lead and rattled off what they wanted. I kept my focus on my pen and pad and collected the menus, not meeting anyone's eyes, then turned back toward the kitchen.

"Wait!" Madison held out a hand but didn't actually touch me. I paused and looked back at her.

"Who cooks the food?" she asked.

Are you fucking kidding me? Couldn't they just let me leave? I glanced at the counter. Leah and one of the other waitresses were throwing me cautious looks. They knew something was up; I was taking too long. I ground my teeth and answered in as calm a tone as I could muster. "Our cook and his assistant."

"So, you don't actually handle the food, right?"

"No." I frowned.

"OK, cool. Just checking. I wouldn't want to catch anything and end up looking like someone took an iron to my face."

The table burst into laughter as I walked off.

I couldn't look at Turner. I didn't think I could hear his deep voice joining in the laughter, but he hadn't defended me either. Maybe he really wasn't the guy I thought he was.

This was the worst night of my life.

I could handle them being assholes to me. This wasn't even as bad as what I usually had to deal with. But the fact that Turner knew everything now, that he'd just sat there and let it happen, that the only people in the world I could remotely call friends had seen me treated like a leper . . . My whole world was imploding, and the rubble was all piling down onto my chest.

As I passed Donna's booth, I couldn't help glancing

up. Half the group was staring at me in shock, the other half studying the table. They were all deathly silent. Donna's gaze bored into me with startling intensity. Was she embarrassed? Upset that I'd made her look bad by association? Was I about to lose every single good thing in my life in one fell swoop?

I rushed away and put the order in, waving off my concerned coworkers with a brittle smile. "Just some kids from my school being dicks. Nothing I can't handle."

We were too busy for anyone to really push the issue.

I did my best to go into autopilot as I delivered the food and drinks to Turner's table in batches. The last was a tray of milkshakes. Once I'd deposited them on the table, Jayden didn't even try to hide the flask as he tipped alcohol into all but one of the frosty glasses. I sighed. There was no point in telling them they couldn't do that. I could tell Leah—she'd kick them all out on their asses. But that would only make things worse for me at school.

I grabbed the tray and straightened up as Madison extended one manicured hand, reaching for the milkshake closest to the table's edge. She nudged it deliberately, like a cat pushing a mug in one of those videos online. I tried to jump back, but it was too late. A strawberry-flavored, icy mess splattered all down the front of my legs and slopped into my shoes.

I gasped as the cold seeped into my clothes.

"Oops." Madison shrugged and pressed her lips

together, fighting a laugh. The whole table was shaking with barely controlled laughter.

"You're so reckless, Phil. I hope that doesn't come out of your paycheck." She tutted, clearly hoping it did. "Oh well. Better bring me another one."

Still not as bad as other shit she'd done to me.

Still Turner did nothing.

Still I couldn't look at him.

Sticky with sugary milk and resentment, I turned to leave.

Amaya and Drew both got to their feet. Drew's hands were balled into fists. Amaya looked ready to explode—her beautiful face had gone red, her eyes bugging out.

My eyes widened, and in a panic, I looked at Donna. She was still seated in the booth, her posture rigid, her intense stare on me. Next to her, Harlow had her head in her hands.

I gave Donna a pleading look and shook my head. It would only make this worse if they made a scene.

"Sit your asses down," she demanded. Drew and Amaya huffed and looked between us, ready to argue. A few of the others had half risen from their seats too, but after a tense moment, they all sat back down.

I hurried off

Leah spotted me. "Oh, shit."

"Yeah." I sighed. "Can someone please send another strawberry milkshake to table twelve? I need to clean up."

"Sure thing, sweetie. Take your time." Leah

squeezed my shoulder as I passed.

In the privacy of the staff bathroom, as I cleaned up as best I could with my shaking hands, I gave in to the tears. They fell freely down my cheeks, fat drops of sorrow, humiliation, and despair. How the hell was I supposed to go back out there and face them all? What the hell was I supposed to do about Turner?

I splashed water on my face even as I continued to sob, the hot tears mingling with the cool liquid. Eventually, I managed to stop crying long enough to dry off. I let my mousy hair down, hoping it would at least partially hide my splotchy face and red eyes.

Fighting fresh tears, I headed back out.

The dinner rush had passed; the diner was half-empty. Table twelve had cleared out.

I breathed a sigh of relief.

Avoiding everyone's eyes, I went to clear it. Madison's group had left an absolute mess and no tip. One plate remained untouched—the cheeseburger with extra fries.

The booth next to it was half-empty too. Donna, Harlow, and Amaya sat in a row on one side, watching me silently.

CHAPTER 11

DONNA HAD BEEN SILENTLY PACING THE length of her massive bedroom for a solid five minutes, her footsteps soft on the luxurious white carpet. She had her arms crossed, a deep frown on her face.

Amaya was leaning against Donna's desk by the window, staring at the floor intently. Harlow was on the bed next to me, her legs drawn up to her chin.

I shifted uneasily, worried about staining Donna's white sheets with my still wet and messy uniform. As if I didn't have enough to obsess over already.

The three of them had stayed in their booth until most of the other customers had cleared out. They hadn't budged while I worked. Only when Leah sent me home, an hour before close, did they get up and follow me outside.

I'd tried to tell them my mom was about to pick me up and I couldn't hang out, but Donna informed me she'd already called my mom and told her I was staying the night at their place. She marched over to her white

BMW and opened the passenger door. I didn't have the energy to argue.

The drive to the nice side of Devilbend—the side with tall gates and trimmed hedges—had been tense and silent. Donna had driven fast, taking corners at unsafe speeds and gripping the steering wheel tightly.

Now we were all piled in her bedroom, several carefully placed lamps casting the opulent space in a warm, soft glow, and still no one had spoken.

My left knee bounced. I couldn't stand not knowing what was going through her head, but I couldn't bring myself to ask. I sighed and leaned my elbows on my knees, digging my nails into my hair.

My movement must've snapped Donna out of it; the sound of pacing stopped. I looked up, my body still bent over itself.

Donna stood in the middle of her room, frowning at me, her hands on her hips. "Mena, what the fuck was that?"

I opened my mouth, no idea how to answer, but what came out wasn't words. It was a sob.

Tears came so quickly and so intensely they took my breath away.

Harlow scooted closer and wrapped her arms around me, while Donna kneeled on the floor and took my hands.

"I'm sorry." Her voice sounded strained.

I glanced at Harlow to see her own eyes were glassy. Amaya was still at Donna's desk, but she was breathing hard, a look of deep worry on her face.

"Mena, I'm sorry." Donna squeezed my hands. "I didn't mean to attack you. I'm just so *angry*. I can't believe those assholes treated you like that. Please, just tell me what's going on."

I took a few shuddering breaths, and even though my heart was in my throat, I told them everything.

The ignoring and exclusion.

The mean comments and taunts.

All the shit on social media—the messages sent to me. At this, Amaya dug my phone out of my bag and demanded my password. I keyed it in, any resistance to them learning the whole ugly truth gone. She scrolled through, her eyes widening, her teeth clenching, her hand eventually covering her mouth in horror.

I told them about the printouts of screenshots when I'd tried to get off social media, about the incident in the bathroom last year. Swallowing any pride I had left, I even told them about Turner. *All of it.* Right up to how he'd done nothing just hours earlier.

I purged it all, laying my dirty, repulsive secrets at their feet to stain Donna's pristine carpet, just as my sticky uniform was staining her sheets.

By the time I'd finished speaking, I was drained, my eyelids heavy, my shoulders slumped. I sighed again and looked around at them.

Silent but steady tears were flowing down Harlow's cheeks. Amaya had one fist pressed to her mouth, her other arm crossed over her chest with my phone still in her hand.

Donna had remained sitting at my feet, her legs

under her, her nails digging into the carpet. "Do your parents know about this?"

"No," I rushed out, her question drawing me out of the numbness I'd fallen into.

"Your teachers? We need to tell—"

"No!" I shot to my feet. "You think I haven't tried? You think I *want* to live like this? You think I haven't gone over every fucking possible way out in my mind? *There is no way out.*"

Donna slowly stood up as I ranted, my hands balled into fists. But it was Amaya who made the next move.

She bolted across the room and smashed into me, squeezing me tightly in her arms. "Oh my god, Mena. *Oh my god!*"

For a beat I just stood there, stunned, my arms hanging at my sides. Amaya was as tough as Donna and even more of a bitch—in a good way. I'd never seen anything get to her. *Ever.* She was stone cold. I couldn't count the number of times I'd wished I was as resilient and cool as her.

I hugged her back, closing my eyes and letting myself be comforted. Donna wrapped her arms around us both, and Harlow completed the group hug on our other side. We just stood like that for a while.

Everything was fucked up beyond measure, but at least I had them. I knew now they didn't simply tolerate me, as I sometimes worried they did; they genuinely considered me as much a friend of theirs as I considered them friends of mine. I wasn't an occasional, annoying, poor fourth wheel in their group. I was *one of them.*

"We love you, Mena." Harlow's voice sounded so small. Had she stopped crying at all? "We've got you, girl. Whatever you want to do, we'll have your back."

"Always," Amaya agreed fiercely, her words right in my ear.

"Without a shadow of a doubt," Donna added. "But, girl, what's the deal with your parents? And the teachers? Why is no one doing anything to stop this?"

"I'll explain," I said. "But . . . er . . . can I do it sitting down? I'm getting kind of hot here, guys."

We all chuckled and separated. We'd been standing in a vertical puppy pile for a good five minutes.

"How about showers first?" Amaya frowned down at her previously white skirt, pulling the fabric away from her perfect legs. Splotches of pale pink marred the pristine fabric.

My eyes widened. "Shit! Sorry, Amaya. I . . ." I was about to say I'd pay for it, but I was pretty certain I couldn't afford to replace that. Maybe I could pay for the dry cleaning.

She fixed me with a firm look. "Stop. You're not allowed to be sorry about anything tonight. I hate this fucking skirt anyway. Go. Shower."

I smiled at her.

"I'll get you some PJs." Donna headed for her closet.

"I'll get us some food." Harlow gave me a watery smile, wiping the tears from her cheeks as she moved toward the door.

After a nice hot shower in Donna's bathroom, with six jets working the tightness from my muscles, I dressed in a bamboo cotton set Donna had left on the bench for me. Somehow, it just happened to be in my size. Harlow and I were about the same height, but I was bigger than all of them—I had a feeling the girls had bought this specifically for me. In fact, I had a feeling they had a whole stash of stuff they were just waiting for an opportune moment to give me.

When I came out of the bathroom, the three of them were pulling a mattress through the door, grunting with the effort.

Harlow flashed me a grin. Her eyes were red, but she'd finally stopped crying. "We're all sleeping in here tonight. It'll be like the slumber parties we used to have when you first moved here."

I shook my head and helped them pull Donna's mattress down too. Her room was spacious enough that we could butt the two mattresses together.

We got comfy in the bedding and pillows, someone put music on, and the next half hour was spent stuffing our faces with junk food. They even had my fave cheddar cheese popcorn. I ate an entire bag by myself and chased it down with chocolate ice cream.

Just as the food coma was setting in, Donna spoke up. "Mena, why don't your parents know about this?"

I sighed. "I've wanted to tell them but . . . what's the point?"

"What do you mean?" Amaya tried to argue. "They're your parents. I'm sure they'd want to—"

"I have no doubt they'd want to help," I interrupted her. "Don't get me wrong—it's not that I think my parents don't give a shit. It's that . . . look, you guys don't understand how much easier some things are when you have money."

They all remained silent. This wasn't something we'd ever discussed, but they weren't idiots. They knew I was poor—as evidenced by the brand-new PJs I was wearing.

"My parents both work full time, and it's just enough to cover our rent, to keep the car running and food in the fridge. When they do overtime, sometimes we can do extra things like go to the movies or get a pizza or whatever. I stopped asking for things a long time ago, because I learned we can't afford them. The only reason I can buy clothes and makeup is because *I* work."

They were listening, but they looked confused, obviously missing the connection.

"If I tell my parents," I went on, "they'll have to come down to the school, talk to my teachers. They'll miss work—money we can't afford to miss out on. And then what? I can't change schools. The only other school that wouldn't take two or more hours to get to is *yours*, and they sure as shit can't afford to send me there. So why stress them out when there's nothing to be done about it?"

"OK." Donna nodded. She was trying to understand, but this was hard for her. She was a doer, a fixer. "They may not be able to let you switch schools, but if they knew the crap you were dealing with, they might be able to get the school to do something about it."

I was shaking my head before she'd even finished.

"No. I've tried. No one gives a shit, you guys." I groaned and ran my hands through my hair. They were all frowning at me.

"What?" Harlow looked outraged.

"When we first moved here, my mom didn't have a job. My dad was working two just to keep us off welfare. They were out of their minds with stress. And when all this crap started . . . it's not like I was bashed up on my first day of school. It started with being excluded, ignored, then the name calling and shit talking started. I went home crying after school for a month solid. On the days my parents were there . . . I didn't have the words to tell them what was happening, and they kind of assumed I was just missing my friends and my old school—that I was struggling to adjust.

"Eventually, I spoke to a teacher. I told Mr. Young that some of the other kids were picking on me. He reminded me of my grandpa with his gut and the bushy moustache." I laughed lightly. "But he all but dismissed me, saying I needed to toughen up, get a thicker skin or some shit.

"When it escalated in sophomore year—the first time Madison shoved me into a wall and then loudly wondered how she'd just bumped into thin air—I reported it to another teacher. We were both called in. Madison denied it, putting on an innocent act. When she left, the teacher said I needed to have proof before accusing other students of serious things. She dismissed it, but Madison sure as fuck didn't. They were careful to stay out of sight of the teachers, but they made my life a living hell for a whole week." I didn't go into details. I didn't like thinking too much about that week, let alone talking about it.

"Anyway," I continued, "a couple of other kids have tried reporting Jayden and his friends too, but it never goes anywhere. The boys are too well liked by the faculty, because they're on the football team. The girls are fucking smart about how they dish out the torture, making it hard to prove. The school can't and won't do anything about it. Trying to report this shit again will just make my life even harder."

"God dammit!" Amaya growled and threw a pillow across the room. "This is infuriating. How the fuck have you been dealing with this for three years, Mena? You're, like, the strongest person I know."

I ducked my head and smiled, flattered. I didn't feel strong. I felt like splinters most days.

"Honestly, you guys, I can handle it," I said.

Disapproving looks fell over their beautiful faces, so I hastened to add, "I know I shouldn't have to. But I can, and there's only, like, 155 school days left before I'm free of it. It was having you guys see it that really upset me tonight." I fiddled with the edge of the cashmere blanket. "I didn't want you to see me like that. I didn't want . . ."

Thinking about him made the lump rise in my throat again.

"You didn't want Turner finding out like this." Harlow squeezed my knee. I nodded, suddenly struggling to meet any of their gazes.

"Fuck Turner!" Amaya crossed her arms. "He can go fuck himself."

I bit back a grin. She was so fierce in her outrage on my behalf. It was downright heartwarming.

"Which one was he?" Harlow asked.

"The one in the baseball cap. Tall, bomber jacket, panty-melting voice, broad shoulders . . ."

Harlow groaned in frustration, and Donna said "fuck" as though she'd just smashed her favorite pair of designer sunglasses.

"Dammit." Amaya shook her head. "Why is it always the hot ones?"

I chuckled, a tiny bit of pride rising in my chest. These beautiful, smart, amazing girls thought my boyfriend was hot. Then I remembered I was pissed at him and didn't know where we stood after tonight, and my face fell.

I checked my phone—nothing. He hadn't even texted to ask if I was OK.

"What are you gonna do about him?" Harlow nudged me with her shoulder.

"I don't know." I shrugged. "Everything is just so fucked up. I want to explain shit. But then I'm so fucking mad he didn't defend me, or even say anything, and he hasn't even texted me. Like, does he even care? But then I think about all the things he's said to me, the *real* connection we have, and I feel like of course he cares! But then after tonight I'm questioning if *that* was even real. Like, what if it was all in my head? What if he knew who I was this whole time, and this is just some

143

elaborate prank? I just . . . I feel like I'm going fucking crazy."

I growled and flopped back against the pillows.

Harlow lowered herself onto her belly next to me, her chin in her hands. "I think you just need to talk to him, get it all out in the open. Maybe he didn't say anything because he was worried it would make it worse for you."

I considered that. He had looked uncomfortable sitting there as they'd picked on me. But that could've been for any reason. Shit, maybe he had gas!

"No. Fuck that," Amaya said, and Harlow rolled her eyes. "Fuck any asshole that isn't there for you no matter what. Ride or die. He didn't ride tonight. So, he should just die. Like, figuratively. In your heart . . . but also maybe literally."

I laughed at her murderous tendencies, then sighed. "Donna? What do you think?"

Donna sat leaning against the bedframe, her legs stretched out and her hands clasped in her lap. She hadn't said anything in a while.

"I think you should sleep on it. Whatever you decide, we'll have your back. And if he hurts you, we'll fuck him up." She was so calm when she said it; I had no doubt my determined cousin would find a way to "fuck up" a guy twice her size. "But honestly, I'm more worried about the shit you're dealing with every day, Mena. You're being bullied, and I can't just stand by and let it happen."

I sat up. "Donna, please. We've been over this. You

can't tell my parents. Or yours. *Please.*" I wasn't above begging.

"I hear you. We won't tell your parents, but you have to let us help."

"What can you possibly do?" I threw my hands up and let them flop onto the soft bedding. I didn't say it— I'd never say it to them—but sometimes their privilege made them think they could just snap their fingers and have whatever they wanted. The real world didn't work like that.

"Maybe we could . . . lean on them a little. Convince them to leave you alone," she suggested vaguely.

I frowned. "What? How?"

"Threaten them. Rough them up a bit." She shrugged, as if it were no big deal. As if she wasn't talking about committing crimes.

Amaya laughed. "OK, Tony Soprano. How are we supposed to do that?"

Harlow was looking at her sister as though she had a screw loose.

"We don't. We get someone else to do it for us. I could make some phone calls," Donna said cryptically.

"To whom?" Harlow chimed in. "We know the same people. None of them are hardened criminals."

Donna looked around at us and smiled. "Uh . . . I'm sure we could find a way. I'm just brainstorming here. We'll figure something out. Point is, Mena, you have to let us help you in some way. I can't just sit around knowing you're being treated like shit. I refuse to do nothing. The Devilbend Dynasty takes care of its own."

There was no point in arguing with Donna when she set her mind to something.

"As long as you promise not to tell our parents or my teachers, and you don't do anything to make my life worse, yes, fine, help away." I sighed and dropped back against the pillows.

CHAPTER 12

WHEN DONNA AND I MANAGED TO DRAG OUR asses out of bed around eleven the next morning, Amaya was already gone, and Harlow was still fast asleep. We made our way downstairs and had breakfast with Auntie Em, then Donna drove me home in relative, comfortable silence. The windshield wipers swooshed rhythmically for the entire twenty-minute drive as a Sunday chill playlist softly drifted through the speakers.

Donna didn't bring up any of the crap we'd discussed ad nauseam the night before until she pulled up next to my building.

"You don't have to deal with this alone anymore, Mena. We're here for you." She gave me a serious look, and I leaned over the console to hug her. She squeezed me tightly, then smiled as I pulled back. "I love you." She looked away.

I appreciated that more than she could know. I knew how hard it was for her to show emotion most of the time.

"I love you too, Donna." I moved to get out of the car, but she reached over and gripped my forearm.

"Let me drive you to school tomorrow." It wasn't a question. It was practically a demand.

I laughed. "Don't *you* have to go to school?"

"Yeah but . . . just let me, OK?"

I narrowed my eyes. "Why?"

She rolled hers. "Mena."

"OK. Fine. I'll see you in the morning."

She finally released my arm. "Great! See ya then."

I got out of the car, and she drove off.

Once she was gone, I trudged up the path toward my building. I'd put my work uniform on to go home, and I didn't really care if I got soaked—it was covered in milkshake anyway.

As I rounded the corner, I paused, my heart flying into my throat.

I hadn't expected to see Turner until tomorrow at school, had maybe even planned to avoid him a while longer. But there he was, sitting on the entryway steps and blocking my way. He had his baseball hat on, his head in his hands, his elbows resting on his knees.

As if he could feel me looking at him, he lifted his head and spotted me. He stood up, his movements lithe and quick, and came down the stairs, out of the cover of the entranceway and into the softly falling rain.

I set my shoulders, lips pursed, and focused on the door, fully determined to walk right past him.

"Mena." He reached for me as I passed. Why did his voice have to sound so rough, so broken?

"Don't touch me." I leapt out of his way, off the path and onto the patchy grass.

He stepped back immediately, his breathing hard, almost frantic. His hands flew to his head before dropping once more to his sides.

Why did he have to look so good? His gray sweatpants hung loose and low on his hips, and a black tank was stretched across his defined chest, the gray hoodie over it left unzipped. I wanted to lean into him, push my hands under the hoodie and around his waist, rest my cheek against his strong chest. How was I supposed to stay mad at him when all I wanted to do was put on my own sweats and find a couch so we could cuddle and listen to the rain?

That rain was now plastering my hair to my face; wet patches were gathering on Turner's shoulders.

I raced up the steps, but he was right on my heels.

"Wait, wait, wait. Mena, please." He sounded so desperate. I hated myself for stopping.

I turned to face him and crossed my arms. "What?"

"I . . ." He looked lost. I could only just make out his eyes under the hat—they were watching me intently, flying about my face. "Fuck. I've been sitting there for hours, running through what I'd say to you, and now it's all just . . . gone."

Hours? "Why have you been sitting in the rain for hours?"

He took a deep breath. "Waiting for you. I waited for you last night too. But then you left with those girls, and . . . I just want to make sure you're OK."

I rolled my eyes. "Whatever. That's why you called and texted last night then? To make sure I'm OK?"

He hung his head. "I wrote and deleted dozens of messages. I was up all night, trying to think of something to say that . . . nothing seemed like it was enough. I . . . I had no idea where to even start."

"A simple 'Are you OK?' would've been a good start."

"Fuck. Yes. You're right. It just seemed so . . . inadequate. I'm sorry. I am *so, so sorry*."

"For what exactly?" I tilted my head, tears stinging the backs of my eyes. This was breaking my heart. He clearly cared. He wouldn't be standing in front of me, looking as torn up as I felt, if he didn't. But I couldn't just let go of the hurt. I wanted answers. Maybe it was unfair to lay all my anger with the world at Turner's feet. But I didn't care what those other assholes had to say—they couldn't hurt me as he could.

"All of it. For what you've had to deal with. For not saying anything last night. For not doing more. For . . . fuck . . . everything. If I'd known it was you all those times, I would've said something. I would've done more. I . . ." He swallowed, faltering, but I still wasn't satisfied.

"That's your reasoning? If you'd known it was me, you would've done something? So, it's not OK that they treat *me* like shit, but it's OK if they do it to other people? Is that the standard, Turner? People you care about should be protected, but fuck everyone else? That's a pretty messed-up morality system. It's *not* OK. Whether it's me or some other desperate loser whose name you don't know, it's not OK to treat people like shit. And it's not OK to stand by and watch it happen and do *nothing*," I ground out and swiped at the angry tears now streaming down my face.

He made a pained sound and reached for me again.

"Don't." I stepped out of his reach, pressing my back against the chipped metal railing.

He turned away, his body radiating tension, and gripped his head with his hands. He took his hat off, ran a hand through his soft blond hair, and put the hat back on backward before turning to face me again.

I had an unhindered view of his face now—could see the dark circles under his eyes, the pain in his dark gaze.

"You're right. It's not OK. You have no idea how badly I want to call them all out on their shit. I don't even fucking *like* Jayden. He is such a douchebag."

"Then why are you friends with them?" I huffed. This was what it came down to. This was why I'd been so afraid to tell him from the start. I was *terrified* he'd choose popularity, image, over something real. Because I no longer doubted what we had was real. I could see it in his desperate eyes, hear it in his pleading voice. He felt as strongly about me as I did about him. But was it enough? Was *I* enough?

He growled and looked up to the ceiling before focusing his gaze back on me. "I don't want to be friends with them. I swear."

"So, stop. We have each other. We're both seniors. School will be over in a few months anyway, and none of this will matter."

He sighed and looked away. "I wish that was true. God, you have no idea how badly I wish that none of this mattered."

My heart splintered.

I wasn't enough.

Fresh tears trailed down my cheeks. I tried to swallow them down, but that just made me choke on my own heartache, so I took a shuddering breath.

Turner's eyes got watery too, and his voice wavered as he spoke. "It's not that simple. I can't just walk away. It's not up to me."

I chuckled darkly and shook my head. "What does that even mean?"

"I don't know how to explain without . . . it's not . . ."

"It's not going to work," I finished for him, dropping my gaze.

"What?" He stepped toward me again, and a sob tore from his throat. "No. That's not . . . just give me a couple of weeks. I need some time to sort it out, and then I'll tell you everything. I can explain all of this. I . . . we can just keep doing what we've been doing. No one has to know. I just need a little time."

He was pleading with me, but it just sounded like more excuses. He wanted to have his cake and eat it too. He wanted to be the gorgeous popular guy everyone liked while still having his piece on the side. Well, I was no one's side chick.

"Fuck you, Turner." I wish I'd said it firmly, with anger lacing the words. But it came out on a sob, sounding weak and hurt—sounding exactly the way I felt.

I wrenched the door open and ran up the stairs, not waiting for the elevator.

He didn't follow me.

CHAPTER 13

ON MONDAY MORNING, FOR THE FIRST TIME, I didn't go out to the balcony and wait for Turner to leave—it didn't matter if he saw me anymore.

Donna's BMW was waiting for me in the same spot where she'd dropped me off the day before. I was honestly glad I wouldn't have to walk to school in the light, unremitting rain.

As soon as I opened the passenger door, I was met with a cheery "Good morning!" that made me cringe. Amaya and Harlow were in the back seat, and all three of them had yelled the greeting. They looked amazing in their Fulton Academy uniforms—teal tartan skirts and matching ties, dark gray blazers over crisp white shirts. I looked down at my skinny jeans and black sweater and sighed.

"It's too early for that level of enthusiasm," I grumbled as I slid into the car. It also made me slightly worried. When they were this coordinated and excited, it usually meant they had something up their sleeve.

"Shut up and caffeinate." Harlow handed over a large takeaway cup.

I moaned before I even tasted it; I could already smell the caramel syrup. They were driving me to school, and they'd gone out of their way to bring me my fave complicated coffee I could in no way afford to have more than once a week. True friendship!

"I'll give you money next time I see you. Don't have my wallet," I mumbled around the cup.

"No, you won't." Donna took off. They always refused to take my money, and I refused to stop offering it.

We chatted about nothing important and listened to music, but it was a short drive. I didn't notice the other cars until they were pulling up next to us.

Another pang of anxiety spiked.

"Shit. What did you guys do?" I bugged my eyes out as a black Lexus pulled up on our left. I could see another shiny, very expensive vehicle beyond. They'd all parked on a diagonal right in front of the school, blocking half the parking lot and taking up space as if they owned it. Who knows, one of them probably did.

I may not have noticed the cars until it was too late, but there was no missing those extravagant vehicles in front of a public school in this area of town. Something was up, and the students wanted to know what. They were slowing down to look, abandoning their trek into the school. Some had even turned back.

"I told you I wasn't going to sit back and do nothing. We're taking care of it," Donna announced.

"Fuck. *What did you do*?" Panic laced my voice. I loved Donna for how fiercely protective she was being, but I worried she was about to make my life even worse.

"I remembered who I was and what I do best," she said, not explaining anything. "Harlow did her creepy online stalker thing to get me the info I needed, and Amaya mobilized the troops. Now it's time to remind them who *you* are."

"Mobilized the . . . guys, this isn't a war." I was fighting to remain calm and failing. No one had gotten out of the fancy cars, and a crowd had started to gather. Hopefully the security guards hadn't noticed the commotion.

"Life is war. And I refuse to lose a single battle." With that final unhinged comment, Donna smoothly got out of the car.

As if they'd been waiting for her move, all the other car doors opened, and suddenly a large group of teal-and-gray uniforms were congregating in the parking lot. Drew, William, and the rest of the crew that had been at the diner the other night were all there, along with what looked like half the Fulton Academy football team.

"Fuck my life." I groaned, took another sip of my sugary coffee, and stepped out of the car.

Several of the Fulton Academy crew waved at me, Nicola gave me a fist bump, and a couple of others gave me hugs. They were just standing in front of the cars and chatting, acting casual—as if it were completely normal for them to be in front of my school twenty minutes before the first bell on a Monday.

"Well . . . uh . . . thanks for the ride, you guys." I kept my voice low, speaking only to the girls. "And the escort, I guess. I'll see ya?" It came out like a question, but I turned to leave anyway.

"Nope." Donna stepped into my path. "We haven't made our point yet."

"What exactly is the point?" It felt as if my heart were trying to shatter my ribcage. So many people were staring, and I hadn't gone unnoticed—the only Devilbend North High student in among all the pretty rich people.

"Just chill." Harlow took my backpack off my shoulder and lowered it to the ground as she and Amaya pulled me back to lean on the hood of Donna's car, positioning me between them.

For lack of anything better to do, I took more sips of my coffee.

"Excuse me." Donna sounded sweet, but I knew that disingenuous tone in her voice. She had her sights set on a freshman, his eyes wide and disbelieving. "Yes, you. Could you please run along and find Madison and Jayden?"

The kid nodded and sprinted toward the school.

Shit, shit, shit. What the fuck was Donna up to? I was dying on the inside. On the outside, I tried to act as cool as they were. "Just those two? I mean, you're here. Might as well get the whole gang together."

"The others will follow." Amaya's face was in her phone, as always, her free hand resting behind me on the car. "It's what they do."

Well, that was ... true, but no less terrifying or panic inducing.

Within a few minutes, excited murmurs rippled through the growing crowd, and a path cleared down the middle. My pounding heart jumped into my throat. I lowered my gaze and hunched my shoulders, taking another sip.

Amaya's hand wrapped around mine. "Head up, Mena. You no longer bow to these vermin."

Her cool, disinterested mask stayed firmly in place, but there was no denying the rage in her tone. Harlow looped her arm through mine, and I took a deep breath and lifted my head. It went against every instinct I had around these people, on these grounds, but I felt stronger with the girls at my side.

Jayden sauntered out of the crowd first, Madison beside him; the others followed close behind, just as Amaya said they would. My gaze scanned their faces, and I wasn't sure whether to be relieved or disappointed when I didn't see Turner with them.

"I hear I've been summoned." Jayden laughed, raising his voice for the crowd, putting on a show. "Color me intrigued. What the fuck do you want?"

Donna smirked at us, then schooled her features into a hard mask, turned to face my tormentors, and crossed her arms over her chest. "Jayden, I'm guessing? And this must be Madison?"

Picking up on Donna's hostile vibe, Madison crossed her own arms and pursed her lips. "And who are you, bitch? What makes you think you can just roll up here and summon us like we're your subjects? This is *our* school. You don't own Devilbend."

"Don't I?" Donna sounded amused. "I'm Mena's cousin, and I thought it was time we had a little chat."

"Who the fuck is Mena, and why should we care?" Jayden chuckled, but his gaze landed on me. They knew what this was about.

"How about you get daddy to buy you a few brain cells and fuck off?" Kelsey snarled, and the girls snickered.

I was screaming internally, not sure if I should be more worried about my safety or Jayden's and Madison's. But I kept my expression smooth, drawing strength from Amaya and Harlow on either side of me.

"You sound and look ridiculous," Bonnie added. "This is the real world. You look like a bunch of preppy losers in those stupid uniforms."

"Our uniform looks better than that tragic Kmart outfit any day." Amaya eyed her up and down.

Bonnie flipped her hair and frowned. "Kmart isn't even a thing anymore. What are you, stupid?"

Amaya just raised her brows and gave her an amused, challenging look, waiting for Bonnie to put two and two together and understand the implication that her outfit not only looked like shit but was outdated.

I could see the exact moment Bonnie figured it out. The smug smile fell off her face, and her nostrils flared, her hands clenching into fists.

"That's enough of the pleasantries." Donna waved a dismissive hand. There was nothing pleasant about her tone—or any of this, really. "Let me put this in a way your subpar-educated, underdeveloped minds will comprehend. My cousin Philomena is—"

"Who the fuck do you think you are?" Madison's raised voice cut across Donna's, but whatever she was going to say died on her tongue.

As one, the entire Fulton Academy crew dropped their casual demeanor. They all pushed off the hoods of their cars and took a menacing step forward, shoulders tense, expressions stony.

My whole body went rigid, ready to spring into action, run away, do *something* when all hell inevitably broke loose. But Amaya and Harlow tightened their hold on me, keeping me in place. Donna didn't even flinch. The four of us were the only ones who didn't move.

As Donna's crew stepped up, the assholes from my school reflexively stepped back, eyes wide in surprise and fear. Some even went into a slight crouch, ready to throw down. The other students gasped, but no one left, too enthralled in the spectacle, the drama. If I hadn't been freaking out, I might have been entertained too— this was better than an episode of *Real Housewives*.

Donna spoke again, her voice clear and firm. "Don't interrupt me when I'm speaking."

She stood still for a beat, letting the silence get heavier.

That's when I noticed Turner. He walked up from the direction of home, his backpack slung over one shoulder and his other hand stuffed into the pocket of his jeans. About halfway into the middle of the crowd, he paused. Every fiber of my being was aware of him in my periphery, but I refused to look directly at him. Plus, I was worried if I took my eyes off Donna, she was going to go full terminator on these fuckers, and that really would complicate my life.

It was like watching an apex predator dominate all the other animals in the jungle. Donna was unflappable, while the others reacted before even thinking shit through.

"Let's try this again," she said. This time, no one dared interrupt. "Philomena Willis is my cousin. I don't allow my family to be treated like shit. So that's going to stop."

"You're trying to force us to be friends with Phil?" Kelsey looked me up and down and sneered.

"Good *god,* no." I could practically hear Donna's eye roll. "No family of mine will lower themselves to your level. No, you're simply to stay away from her. Don't talk to her. Don't touch her. Don't contact her online. Don't so much as think about her."

"Or what?" Jayden was brave enough to step forward, I'd give him that. Or maybe I was mistaking bravery for stupidity.

"Or there will be consequences," Donna said, as if she were explaining something complicated to a toddler.

"Are you threatening us?" Madison sounded outraged.

"No. I'm simply explaining cause and effect. Fuck with Mena and I'll fuck with you." For the first time, a bit of bite entered Donna's tone.

"How full of yourself can you be?" Madison crossed her arms again, but she was staying back, in the relative safety of the crowd. "None of you assholes go here. You can't protect her all the time."

She threw me a smug look, and my heart sank. I refused to let it show on my face, but this was exactly what I was afraid of. The Fulton crew would all drive off, go back to their privileged lives, and I'd be left to deal with the pack of animals they'd just poked with a proverbial stick. What the hell was Donna thinking?

But I should've known. Donna never did anything without thinking it through. Without at least three backup plans.

"That's cute." I could hear the smirk in Donna's voice. "Your world is so tiny. But that's the thing. You feel powerful in a pack, pushing a girl around, walking these halls like you own this school. But there's a whole big world out there. A world in which your parents live and work. A world in which I can ruin you in more ways than you can count."

"Empty words." Jayden scoffed. "My dad works for BestLyf. You're not the only one who knows people."

"Your father—Boyd Burrows—is middle management at best. He doesn't even make enough to send you to a private school."

How the hell did she know his dad's name? I frowned, and Harlow chuckled, giving my arm a little squeeze. Of course. Harlow's stalking. But I didn't have time to think about how creepy my little cousin could be. Donna was still speaking.

"And, Bonnie, your mom works at GoodGrocer, right? Heath Preston owns that company. He and my dad are old friends. I call him Uncle Heath. And, Steph, your dad works for Mitchell Mechanics. Mr. Mitchell went to college with my mom. We had him and his wife, Darlene, over for dinner last week. Oliver Vanderford runs Norton Corp. He and my dad are golf buddies—he even tried to set me up with his son a few times." She chuckled, then got deathly serious again. "Several of your parents work for him, right? I'd hate to have to mention to my family friends how *appallingly* their employees' children are behaving. I mean, these are family-run, respectable businesses. They can't have people working for them who would tarnish those brands."

Holy. Shit. Most of the kids at my school were in similar situations to mine. We knew how tenuous our parents' grip on financial stability was. Donna had gone right for the jugular. I almost felt sorry for them.

They all looked furious, teeth clenched, eyes narrowed. But how could they argue with that?

Then Kelsey stepped forward and propped a hand on her hip. "My parents work for themselves. You can't do shit to threaten me. You don't control everything, you stuck-up bitch."

For the first time since she'd started to speak, Donna moved. She took three measured steps forward, leaned in, and whispered in Kelsey's ear.

Kelsey visibly paled. Her eyes widened and looked at Donna with fear. "You can't ... how ..." she stammered, then turned on her heel and barreled through the crowd.

I'd never wanted anything as badly as I wanted whatever that information was—the ability to make Kelsey disappear like that? *Priceless.*

Donna raised her voice. "That's all. Dismissed."

She turned back to us, a satisfied smile on her face as the crowd all started to speak over one another.

"Remind me to never get on your bad side." I gave her a tentative smile.

"Shit, I'm your sister, and I'm a little scared." Harlow chuckled.

"I'm kinda turned on." Amaya cocked her head, and we all burst out laughing.

"Thank you, guys. I really hope this works." I gave them each a hug.

"Anytime, girl. We got you." Donna held on for an extra beat before letting go.

And then I was swallowed in a sea of Fulton uniforms as every single person Donna had brought with them came up and gave me a hug, a fist bump, or words of encouragement murmured in my ear.

Drew stepped up last, that cheeky grin on his face, and wrapped his big arms around me. His tight squeeze lifted me clean off the ground, eliciting a surprised yell from me that ended on a laugh. My legs hung limply as my arms held on to his neck.

"I'm sorry this shit is happening to you, Mena," he whispered in my ear.

"Me too," I whispered back. "Thanks for having my

back. I really appreciate it."

"You got it. It was fun, actually." He dropped me to my feet and grinned before saying goodbye and rushing for his car.

Most of the crowd had dispersed while my protectors were taking their leave, but Jayden still stood in the same spot, arms crossed, glaring.

It wasn't until the cars started to pull away, their powerful engines roaring and purring, that he sneered and walked off.

I really fucking hoped this wouldn't make everything worse. Now that my defenders were gone, I was alone again, and that thought sent a cold chill of fear down my spine.

I dropped my empty coffee cup in the trash and picked my bag up off the ground. As I straightened, I noticed Turner still in the same spot, hands in his pockets. He was staring after the cars as they pulled away, his strong brow deeply furrowed.

He kind of looked as if he wanted to punch something—or someone. I knew the feeling. I just couldn't figure out what his problem was. He refused to stand up for me, but no one else was allowed to either?

His gaze turned to me, and the deep, angry frown cleared. The look in its place was kind of uncertain. If I didn't know better, I'd say it was longing that stretched across the distance between us.

He took a deep breath, readjusted his bag on his shoulder, and took a few steps in my direction.

Then his eyes caught on something over my

shoulder, and he stopped with a frown. And just like that, I was forgotten again. He changed direction and speed-walked toward the school entrance.

I turned just in time to see Jenny—skinny arms wrapped around her torso, head hung low—walk around the corner of the building. Turner wasn't heading for the entrance. He was going after Jayden's little sister.

In all the bullshit that had been happening lately, I'd almost forgotten that weird situation. Part of me wanted to go after them, demand answers. I'd had enough of this shit. But I was also exhausted, bone tired in every way possible, and it wasn't even nine on Monday morning.

The bell sounded, making the decision for me, and my thoughts turned back to what I would meet beyond those doors.

Donna had bluffed those assholes like a pro. There was nothing left to do but borrow her limitless confidence, keep the bluff going, and walk in there with my head held high.

CHAPTER 14

THE NEXT THREE DAYS WERE BLISSFULLY uneventful. Donna and the girls got up extra early and drove me to school every morning, my sweet caramel concoction ready for me as soon as I got in the car. I walked into school and went to my classes with my shoulders back and eyes up. No one bothered me. I still kept to myself and had lunch on my own—I wasn't expecting Donna's threats to work miracles—but I no longer slunk through the halls like a wounded animal. Jayden and Madison sneered when I passed, but the rest of them just ignored me. Kelsey actively avoided me, turning to rush in the other direction whenever she saw me coming.

I'd tried to get Donna to tell me what she'd whispered to her, but she just smirked and cryptically replied that "Secrets like that only have power while they're still secret."

Figuring it was Harlow who'd dug up the dirt on some shady part of the internet, I asked her, but she was just as mystified as me. Whatever it was, Donna had found it all on her own.

Turner kept his distance. He didn't call or text, and I avoided the balcony, so I had no idea if he was going out there or not. It was so damn hard to stay away from him. I couldn't count the number of times I'd written a text only to delete it, had reached for the sliding door handle before pulling myself away. I cried about it every night, when everyone was asleep and the house was dark and silent. I missed him like crazy, and knowing he was just on the other side of the wall was torture.

But it had to be like this. Donna and the girls had lit a fire under me, and I was rolling with this newfound self-confidence thing. I couldn't be with someone who was ashamed to be seen with me.

But I also couldn't really figure out what he was thinking. He'd all but stopped hanging out with that group, though he did walk the halls with Jayden from time to time, and they still talked as if they were close in English. Turner's presence directly in front of me in that class made it impossible to focus. Now that I knew I'd never touch him again, reaching out and feeling his firm, warm shoulder under my palm was all I could think about.

I caught him looking at me several times a day, his expression neutral but his eyes blazing with perplexing emotion.

I'd also seen him speaking with Jenny two more times. Whatever they were up to, they were getting careless. But I was no longer worried he was doing something shady—something to hurt the fragile girl. She looked as if she was pleading with *him* now, and the last time I spotted them by the stairs, she'd even leaned forward and given him a tentative hug. Turner had frozen for a moment, then wrapped his big arms around her little frame and patted her shoulder gently. The gesture looked protective more than anything. I'd left more confused than ever.

By the time my Thursday night shift came around, I was exhausted from the week's emotional whiplash but feeling hopeful. There was only one day left before the weekend. I'd nearly made it.

"So, I'm going to speak to Leah tomorrow"—Chelsea leaned in, keeping her voice low as we wrapped napkins around cutlery—"but I just wanted to tell you I'm going to quit."

I dropped a knife, and it clattered on the counter. "What? Why?"

"I'm gonna miss working with you too, Philly. You were really there for me after the breakup and all that. But it's time." She smiled at me serenely, but my frown only deepened.

"Time for what? Did you get another job?"

"No. But I can't expect amazing things to happen when I'm wasting my time and energy on mediocre things. I learned that at my last BestLyf seminar. I feel really positive about the future."

Mediocre things like making money to buy food and pay rent? I wished I had the confidence to say that to her, but we weren't that close. Instead I just sighed and added Chelsea's quitting to the long list of shit my mind was struggling to deal with. Two large groups came in right after she told me, so I didn't have a chance to ask her more about it anyway.

I got off about ten, texted my dad to pick me up, then grabbed my stuff from the back room. Before leaving, I tried to talk to Chelsea again about her decision, but she waved me off and went to clear one of the remaining tables.

With a sigh, I stepped out into the crisp night air.

"Mena?"

I'd have recognized Turner's ocean-deep voice anywhere. I was pretty sure I'd go to my grave knowing exactly what my name sounded like on his lips. I squeezed my eyes shut and steeled myself before turning toward him.

He stepped away from the wall, out of the shadows. His hat was obscuring his eyes, his dark hoodie and jeans only adding to the menacing vibe.

"What are you doing here?" I asked, unsure if my heart was beating faster because he'd startled me or because I was excited to see him.

"I need to talk to you. You haven't been coming out to the balcony, so . . ."

"So you decided to wait for me at my work like a creep? You could've talked to me at school. You could've called me."

"Would you have picked up?" He conveniently ignored the bit about being seen with me at school.

"I don't know that there's anything left to say,

Turner. You made your choice."

"No, I didn't." He stepped toward me, reaching his arms out. "And I have a lot to say. I want to tell you everything. I can't do this anymore. I miss you so much."

His words snaked into my chest, wrapped themselves around my heart and squeezed.

"Why are you doing this? Just let me get over you." *As if I could.*

"Well, *I* can't get over *you,* so . . . I don't even want to." He took a breath and another step closer, visibly steadying himself before speaking again. "Look, I have a lot to explain. Can I please just walk you home?"

I checked my phone—my dad would be there any minute. "Turner, I can't . . ."

"Please."

"No. My—"

"She's my sister," he rushed out just as familiar headlights turned the corner, my dad's beat-up old Toyota Corolla heading straight for us. "Jenny is my little sister."

"What?" I frowned, my brain trying to process. What the hell was he talking about? Was this some attempt to confuse me even further, somehow manipulate me into getting back together with him?

Dad's car pulled up, and Turner closed his mouth, abandoning whatever lie he'd been about to spew next.

"My dad's here. I have to go," I gritted out and turned for the car. Dad rolled down the window, the glass making an obnoxious squeaking noise, and leaned over to look at us. "Hey, Philly. Who's your friend? Do you need a lift anywhere, son?"

I bugged my eyes out at my dad as I opened the passenger door, and he gave me a little frown. When I turned to put my belt on, I jumped. Turner had followed me to the car and was leaning down to look through the window, a friendly expression on his face. I narrowed my eyes at him, but it was too late.

"Actually, I live in your building, sir, and I'd really appreciate a lift." He smiled.

My dad ignored my death glare completely. "Sure thing. Jump in."

I huffed and stared out the window, ignoring them both. The radio was on some easy-listening station, Michael Bublé's crooning the only thing breaking the awkward silence.

After a few minutes, dad eyed the rear-view mirror. "Hey, you—dark and brooding in the back seat. What's your name?" He chuckled at his own mortifying joke.

I only just resisted the urge to pinch the bridge of my nose.

"Turner Hall, sir."

"Nice to meet you, Turner. I'm Brad."

"Nice to meet you too, sir."

After another few awkward minutes of silence, Dad cleared his throat. "Soooo, how do we know Turner, Philly?"

I growled under my breath. I really wished they'd stop calling me Philly, especially in front of people. I was *Mena*. And I wasn't about to explain to my dad the clusterfuck that was Turner and me. "He goes to my school."

Turner sighed, clearly not happy with how I'd reduced our relationship to "classmates," but Turner could go fuck himself. At least he was smart enough to remain silent.

"Cool." Dad dragged the word out and turned the music up, but we were already pulling into the parking area at the back of the buildings.

We piled out of the car, and Turner turned to my dad. "Thank you for the lift, Mr. Willis."

"You're welcome." Dad thumped him on the shoulder. "And please, call me Brad."

Were they trying to be chummy? *Ugh!* That time I couldn't stop my hand from reaching up to pinch the bridge of my nose. I walked to the entrance without looking at either of them.

"Mena?" Turner's pleading tone made me turn to face him. He was begging me with his eyes.

I hated myself for it, but I was curious. With a defeated shake of my head, I turned to my dad. "I'll be up soon, Dad. Just need to speak to Turner."

Dad paused, one hand on the door handle, and looked around at the parked cars, the tall apartment buildings. "I don't know if you noticed, but we live in kind of a rough neighborhood. It's getting late." As if to emphasize his point, a car alarm went off somewhere in the distance, and several dogs started barking in response.

Turner climbed the few steps to join us on the

landing. "I'll keep her safe, sir."

Dad gave him a long, serious look. "I'm not entirely convinced she doesn't need to be kept safe *from* you."

My lips twitched into an almost smile. I was simultaneously mortified and kind of happy Turner was copping shit from someone.

"I swear to god, I would never hurt a hair on Mena's head."

"No, you just stand by and watch other people do it," I cut in.

Dad's hard gaze turned on me, his brows creasing in a worried frown. "Philomena?"

I took a calming breath and gave him a reassuring smile. "It's fine, Dad. I'll be up soon."

He looked between us with narrowed eyes. "If you're not up there in fifteen, I'm coming back down." And because he was a dad, and by default an embarrassment, he raised his digital watch, pressed a few buttons on it, and showed us the timer ticking down before he disappeared into the building.

Turner and I stared at each other until the sound of my dad's footsteps faded. Then his mouth quirked up on one side. "Philly?"

"Seriously?" I ground out through clenched teeth. "If you're going to poke fun at me, I'm just gonna go."

I reached for the door, but he lunged forward and took my elbow. "No. Wait. I'm sorry. I just . . . I miss you. I miss our banter."

"Yeah, well . . ." I extracted my arm from his grip. "You said you wanted to talk, not banter, so . . . what the fuck do you mean Jenny is your sister?"

He blew out a big breath and took his hat off, putting it on backward. I wasn't sure if it was better or worse now that I could see the desperation in his gaze. "OK, fair enough. I meant what I said. She's my sister. But no one here knows that. That's why I've been speaking to her, and that's why it looks kind of intense when I do. We've ... been through some shit. About three years ago, my mom and my sister left, disappeared. My dad and I have been looking for them ever since."

"What? That doesn't even make sense. This sounds like some ridiculous story you made up to confuse me. I just can't understand *why*."

Turner sighed. "I'm not making shit up. I wish I were."

He looked resigned, kind of sad, as he pulled out his phone, tapped away at it, and then held it out to me. Staring back at me from the screen was a young Turner. He was skinnier, a bit more gangly, but it was definitely him grinning at the camera, his arm slung around a little girl's shoulders. I frowned; the girl definitely looked like Jenny.

"Flick through. There's more." Hands in his pockets, he stepped up next to me so we could both look at the pictures on the screen. The next was of a couple, arms around each other, the man laughing while the woman looked off to the side. I'd seen Turner's dad a few times, and that was unquestionably him in the pic—the woman had to be Turner's mom. The next photo showed all four of them grouped around a cake with several candles, Jenny the center of attention at what looked like a birthday celebration. The next was of Turner and his mom. Photo after photo of what was clearly his family.

"I don't understand." I handed the phone back. "What exactly happened? And what does this have to do with anything?"

Turner checked the time. "Look, I don't know how much time we have before your dad's countdown clock runs out, but I'll try to keep it brief. Like I said, my mom took my sister and left. She tried to take me too, we got into a huge fight, and I went and stayed the night at a friend's. I had no idea she was intending to just disappear."

I held up a hand to stop him. "Wait a second. If your mom took your sister, isn't that, like, some form of kidnapping? Why didn't your dad just go to the police?"

"Of course he did. They checked with a few of my mom's friends from church and the one cousin who was all the family we had in the area, then pretty much told him there was nothing they could do. That was just before they put me into a room and asked me a bunch of leading questions about whether my dad got angry or drank or ever yelled at my mom. They pretty much just assumed he was abusive and she'd run away from him. They told him to get a lawyer and washed their hands of it—wouldn't even hear him out about the people responsible. The people that have been helping her stay hidden."

"What people?" I checked my phone. We had ten minutes.

"Look, my parents did not have a happy marriage. I mean, maybe they did when I was younger—I do remember some happy times. But by the time I was in my teens, they'd just fallen out of love. They argued from time to time, and things were tense, distant. But my dad was never abusive. I never once saw him hit her or throw anything or even raise his voice. They weren't at each other's throats—they were just making each other miserable. I think they were trying to keep the family together for us kids, but I wish they'd just broken up. Maybe all this could've been prevented then.

"Anyway, the point is, my mom was lonely, broken. Looking back on it, she had some issues—things neither she nor my dad were equipped to deal with. Those things made her vulnerable. She somehow got mixed up with these BestLyf people, started going to a few free meetings. Then she started paying to attend the more intense seminars. That caused more arguments about money. Dad thought she was wasting it, and Mom felt like it was the only good thing in her life."

"What exactly are you saying?" A heavy dread settled in my gut. I believed he was telling the truth about Jenny being his sister—the photos were undeniable. And I believed him when he said his dad wasn't abusive. I'd never heard any yelling or crashing from the apartment next door, and Turner had never said or done anything to make me think he was scared of his dad. But the story just kept getting crazier and crazier.

"I'm pretty sure BestLyf is a cult." He propped his hands on his hips.

I frowned. That couldn't be right, could it? My mom went to those meetings and had nothing but good things to say. Chelsea loved every second of the personal-development courses. Cults didn't help people be their best selves—they made you live on some secluded farm, waiting for the second coming or some shit. Didn't they?

"What are you talking about? BestLyf is a corporation. They have offices all over the country. They advertise on TV, for fuck's sake." Was Turner a conspiracy theorist?

"I know it sounds crazy, but we're not the only ones this has happened to. There's a whole network of people who have lost loved ones to that hellhole."

"Then did you report that to the police? I'm pretty sure cults are illegal."

"We did." He sounded defeated. I wanted to hug him, so I stuffed my hands into the pockets of my apron. "But after the fifth police station my dad was laughed out of, he stopped trying. BestLyf is a legitimate business in the front—they do provide legit services, but they hide behind that front and ruin people's lives. They've been at this for years. It's hard to find proof. We couldn't get any help from the police, so Dad went straight to the source. He banged on the doors of the BestLyf office in our town, demanded to see my mother. They denied she'd ever even attended a meeting. When we realized my mom and sister were no longer even in town, we started looking for them elsewhere.

"Dad did some research and found all the places they have offices, training facilities, retreats—any property that's associated with them. And we started going to these places. Dad tried to get jobs with them in different towns, but they obviously communicated well between branches, and he could hardly step onto the property before they would call security. So, we came up with a new strategy. We would go to a town where BestLyf had an office, Dad would get a job doing whatever he could find, and I would be enrolled in the local school. I'd make friends, talk to people, figure out whose parents worked for BestLyf, and try to get some inside info. Every spare second we had, we'd stake out the offices and employees' houses trying to get a glimpse of my mom and sister. When we were sure they weren't in that town, we'd move on to the next one."

My eyes widened as he told his insane yet somehow admirable story. I couldn't believe the lengths they were going to. But then, maybe I could. Who knows what I'd do for my own family? "Holy shit," I breathed. "And now you've found them."

"And now we've found them."

I turned away, threading my hands into my hair. "This is fucking insane, Turner."

"I know," he rushed out. "But this is *why*. Please, you have to believe me. This is the only reason I put up with that bunch of cunts. I want to punch Jayden in the nose half the time. But pretending to be his friend has allowed me to get closer to Jenny. I've been over to his place a few times and managed to snoop around a bit. They did a number on my sister, and she's refusing to see my dad, but she hasn't told anyone we're here, so I have hope she's starting to come around. They've convinced her my dad was a bad man—that he was the reason my mom took her and left. I'm slowly helping her remember. But we still haven't seen any sign of my mom, and any time I ask her, Jenny clams up."

"What about Jayden? Have you asked him?"

"About my mom?" He sighed in frustration. "I can't really ask him directly without giving away who I am. I've tried to bring it up in a roundabout way—asking if his mom or dad will be home when he invited the boys over, or asking what his mom does when he mentioned his dad's work. That kind of thing. But all he's said is that his mom died when he was eleven, and he doesn't like talking about it. Never even mentioned a stepmom or anything. It's so fucking weird."

He was breathing hard, his shoulders tight and his fists clenching as he talked. I wanted to wrap my arms around him and make it all better.

"I can't blow my cover yet," he went on. "I can't risk them finding out who I am or that we're even here. But having you think I don't care is fucking tearing me up inside. So, I'm trusting you, Mena. I'm trusting you with my truth."

I hadn't trusted him with mine.

He didn't say it, and I didn't think he meant to throw that in my face, but I drew the parallel myself. I'd lied to him to protect myself. He'd lied to me to protect his family.

And he was dealing with so much—an insurmountable, crazy amount of pressure.

I couldn't hold back anymore. I rushed forward and wrapped my arms around his waist. He hugged me back hard, his heart hammering under my cheek, his heavy breath in my hair.

My phone rang, and I hurried to answer it—it had been twenty minutes. "Just waiting for the elevator, Dad," I said before he could even speak.

"You better be in this apartment in the next three minutes, Philomena."

"Yes. I'm coming." I hung up without waiting for a response and stepped out of Turner's embrace. It was harder than I could've imagined—to have his arms around me after so much angst about how he really felt . . . "I have to go."

He nodded, but he looked so uncertain. "Are we good?"

"Honestly, I don't know. This is just . . . a lot. I need to process."

"OK. Yeah, of course. Just promise you'll let me know if you have any questions? I'll tell you whatever you want to know."

I nodded. I had no more words.

But Turner did. "I want you to know I'm going to

fight for you. I know you need to think about all this, but I can't lose you. You're the best fucking thing that's happened to me in a long time."

With one last agonizing look at his beautiful, tortured face, I left.

CHAPTER 15

AS WAS BECOMING MY NEW NORMAL, I HARDLY slept that night. Thinking about Turner used to keep me up with giddy excitement as I replayed all our interactions in my head. Lately, Turner kept me up because I was heartbroken over how shit had gone down, first because he didn't seem to care and now because of his supposed tragic story.

Around two in the morning, I gave up and grabbed my phone, hardly even surprised when I saw Harlow was online. That girl kept the weirdest times. On a whim, I messaged her. I didn't feel right telling her Turner's story—it felt too private and heavy, with too much at stake if it was true—but I couldn't just take his word for it. Even though I couldn't go into details, Harlow helped me anyway. She dug up a few local missing-person articles from three years ago, and when she looked into Turner's dad, she couldn't find anything worrying, other than complaints from BestLyf.

It all matched Turner's story.

I managed to get maybe three hours of sleep before my alarm went off, and when I saw myself in the mirror, I groaned. I looked like shit. With the girls having my back, and Madison and the others having left me alone all week, I was just emboldened enough to apply some eye makeup. Nothing ostentatious—just enough to cover the bags under my eyes. I didn't touch my birthmark, figuring it was best not to draw too much attention to the fact that I was wearing makeup.

Mom asked over breakfast if I could do her makeup that night. It was my aunt and uncle's anniversary party.

I shook my head. "Sorry. Gotta work. Have fun."

"OK, sweetheart. I'll just pick your dad up and head straight there after work then, so we won't see you after school. Drive dad's car to work—don't walk, OK?"

I waved her off, yawning as I headed out the door.

The girls drove me to school, and the giant coffee they brought me helped perk me up a bit. Thankfully, Harlow didn't bring up our late-night sleuthing. I still wasn't sure what to do about that, or how to feel about it.

I made it through most of the day in a haze, hardly paying attention in class and nearly nodding off in English. As I stopped at my locker during lunch, Madison and her friends happened to be walking past. I spared them a glance and ignored them, assuming they'd keep doing what they'd been doing all week—leaving me alone.

How wrong I was . . .

Madison's eyes narrowed as she took in my face, and she walked straight up to me. Kelsey turned around and hurried off, but that still left three of them hovering around my locker.

Madison leaned in and sneered. "You can slap all the makeup on it you want, but you'll always be ugly, Phil."

Anger rose quickly and unchecked, and I slammed my locker shut. I was so done with everything the past few months had thrown at me.

"What the fuck is your problem?" I got up in her face and did not keep my voice down, did not cower or back away. I was like a different person, hands thrown out and eyebrows raised as I unleashed. "What did I ever do to you? Seriously? Why do you hate me so much? Why do you care?"

She shrugged, but the gesture lacked her usual nonchalance. She was seething. "There's just something about certain people. You can't really put your finger on it, but you can't stand the sight of them. You're just hateable, and I wish you'd do me a fucking favor and just die."

"You're a hateful, spiteful bitch, and you'll never be happy. Go fuck yourself!" I yelled into her face. I was completely lost in the rage, not thinking at all about the words coming out of my mouth.

"Miss Willis." Mr. Chen's deep voice froze me to the spot. All the fight drained out of me, and my face fell as I slowly turned toward my English teacher.

He had his hands on his hips, his expression very

stern. "That kind of language is unacceptable."

"You should've heard what she was saying before you got here, sir." Suddenly, Madison sounded meek, her voice even a little watery. "She called me the most awful things."

"It's true, sir. We heard it all," Bonnie piped in, Steph nodding emphatically.

What a joke. I rolled my eyes. "Please. What about all the things you've said to me over *literally years.*"

Madison gasped and pressed her hand to her chest. "I would never—"

"Enough!" Mr. Chen snapped, taking his glasses off and rubbing his eyes with the heel of his hand. He looked about as tired as I felt as he mumbled under his breath— something about shitty pay and long hours and teenagers being the devil.

"Miss Barnes, I heard the terrible things you said too. Now, I don't know what this is about, and I don't want to." He held his hand up, stopping Madison from spewing another lie. *Of course* he didn't want to know about it. None of the teachers gave a shit. "You're both about to be adults. You're seniors, for god's sake. The younger kids look up to you. Start acting like it."

"Yes, sir." Madison nodded.

"I'm sorry." I sighed.

"I'm not done," he barked, then looked between us. "Detention. Both of you. You can take the time to think about what it means to conduct yourself with dignity. I'll see you both this afternoon."

He walked off without another word.

All three of them stared daggers at me. If this were a cartoon, steam would have been coming out of Madison's ears. I flipped them off and walked away, hoping to spend the last twenty minutes of lunch taking a nap in the library. This really sucked ass. I'd have to run home, grab my uniform, and head straight to work.

Mr. Chen slept through most of detention, leaning back in his chair with his mouth hanging open. It suited me just fine, as I was able to doze a bit too, although it was hard to fall asleep completely with Madison sending me a death glare from across the room, stopping only to text on her phone.

The moment Mr. Chen's alarm went off at the end of the hour, he eagerly dismissed us and hurried ahead out the door, his shoes echoing in the empty hall. I tried to rush off too, but Madison kept getting in my way, slowing me down until the other students were all ahead of us too.

As we neared the corner around which were the front doors—and my freedom from this nightmare of a day—the door to the last classroom flew open. I gasped, but before I could make another sound, a hand covered my mouth, and several others pulled me into the dark room. Madison calmly stepped in after us, closing the door with a quiet *click*.

My pulse thudded in my ears as I struggled, kicked my legs, threw my head from side to side to try to dislodge the hand over my mouth.

Had the others already walked out the door? Was

anyone still around to hear me scream? *Oh god!* My parents weren't even home to notice I hadn't come home.

Panic choked me as I redoubled my struggling, its icy grip cutting off my air as badly as the hand over my face. I screamed anyway. The sound was pitiful, muffled by my attacker's hand.

"Would you shut her up?" Madison hissed. She was still by the door, listening, peering out, making sure we were alone.

Steph stepped into my field of vision and punched me in the gut. Her arms were as weak and useless as mine, so the blow didn't make me double over in pain, but it still hurt, startled me, made me cough.

The hand over my mouth disappeared. "Ugh! Gross! She slobbered all over me," Jayden complained.

I took a deep breath and screamed as loudly as I could.

Bonnie rushed over and slapped me, cutting the sound off and snapping my head to the side. Jayden's firm grip on my arms kept me upright.

"Shut the fuck up, you whore," Madison growled as my cheek burned.

For a few seconds, the only sound was my ragged breathing, bouncing off the abandoned walls of the dark classroom. There were no running footsteps out in the hall, no worried cries—no one had heard me scream.

No one was coming.

I swallowed back the fear threatening to take over and took a deep breath. I needed to stay calm. I needed to get myself out of this.

Madison was still by the door, and Jayden was still holding me, his grip on my upper arms sure to bruise. He seemed to be the only guy.

Kelsey wasn't with them. Whatever Donna had on her must've been way heavier than threatening poor people's jobs—and that had been going straight for the throat. Which begged the question . . .

"Why are you doing this?" My voice was croaky, weak. "What the hell are you thinking?"

"Your stuck-up cousin's threats spooked people, but we talked it over, and . . ." She shrugged. "I don't believe her. I mean, she's a senior in high school, just like us. As if she could really get anyone fired."

I chuckled darkly and shook my head. Clearly, they didn't know Donna. But laughing was the wrong move.

Another slap stung my cheek, and Madison leaned in close, baring her teeth. "Who the fuck does she think she is, coming here and threatening us? Who the fuck do *you* think you are? You're not one of them. You're poor, sad, worthless trash. And you need to be reminded of it."

Did she realize she'd just put us in the same category? That she'd all but referred to *herself* as worthless trash?

It probably wasn't wise to laugh again though. That last hit had cut the inside of my cheek, and the taste of coppery blood filled my mouth.

Steph poked her head out the door and looked up

and down the corridor. "No one's around. Let's get moving." She walked out of the room, and the others followed, Jayden pulling me along roughly.

Where were they taking me? What were they going to do to me? They'd never gone this far. Even the incident with the mop hadn't made me bleed, and it felt as if they were just getting started.

CHAPTER 16

IN THE WEEK AFTER DONNA'S SHOW, I ALMOST couldn't believe how well it had worked. They had really been leaving me alone. It was all I'd ever wanted. She'd pushed them into a corner and made it clear it was either submit to her demands or be ruined.

But that's the thing—when animals are pushed into a corner, the only thing they can do is fight. Madison and her crew were fighting, all right. But four against one wasn't exactly fair.

As we rushed through the dark hallways of the school, I tried to scream another few times, but one of them would always shove me or smack me over the head; they didn't seem too worried about it. They knew just as well as I that everyone had gone home.

I'd have to figure out some way to save *myself*. Whatever I had in my bag was useless, sitting as it was in the empty classroom where I'd dropped it. The only thing I had on me was my phone, tucked into the back pocket of my jeans. All I could do was hope they didn't discover it, and wait for a moment when I could call for help.

At the doors leading out to the football field, they paused again, checking that the coast was clear. Then we were making our way across the grass, which was still wet from the previous night's rain. The bluish-gray light of dusk covered everything in a gauzy blanket of shadows, and the chill wind raised goosebumps along my forearms.

Out in the open, I hoped there might be someone around to hear me, so I screamed again.

Jayden shoved me to the ground. The impact cut off my scream, pushing all the air out of my lungs.

"Shut the fuck up!" he roared above me, one foot on either side of my hips. "Scream again and I'll knock out all your teeth." He turned to Madison and threw his arms out. "What the fuck are we doing, Madison? This bitch isn't worth it."

Madison's tone was clipped, her rage barely restrained. "Get her ass up and get her to that goal post, now. I refuse to be threatened by her. She needs to learn a lesson she'll never forget."

Jayden sighed but did as he was told, dragging me up roughly by the arm.

They'd completely lost the plot. She was so outraged I'd dared to step out from under her control, so angry with the world and her place in it, she was lashing out. She wasn't even thinking about the consequences. All she could see was *red*.

I'd never been more scared in my life.

This wasn't about humiliating me in front of the rest of the school.

This went deeper.

"Against the pole." Madison pointed, and Jayden slammed me into the goalpost, my back crunching.

The other girls disappeared behind me and yanked my arms back. A cable tie zipped into place around my wrists.

"What do we have here?" Steph taunted as she pulled my phone out of my back pocket. I closed my eyes and sighed. That was my only chance . . .

She held it by one corner and waved it in front of my face, smirking.

Bonnie grabbed it, threw it on the ground, and stomped on it, the screen making a devastating cracking sound under her foot. "Who the fuck would you have to call anyway?"

My eyes went wide. I knew they could do serious harm to me, was preparing myself for it. But with my hands tied to the pole and no way out, for the first time, I wondered if they were about to kill me.

The panic I'd been holding back broke through, and I started crying. Sobs racked my body, and tears trailed down my cheeks.

"Please," I wailed. "Please, just let me go. No one has to know. I won't even tell Donna. Just let me go, and we can pretend this never happened."

Bonnie spat at my feet as Madison mimicked me. "Please, please, don't hurt me. Wah!" She ended on a cruel laugh, which her sadistic friends echoed. "Like I give a shit if you tell Donna. Like I give a shit what you want."

She stepped forward and shoved her thumb against my right eye. I closed it just in time, but she didn't try to gouge it out as I expected. Instead, she dragged her thumb down my cheek, smearing the makeup.

She cocked her head, surveying her work as more tears poured out of me. "There. That's more like it. Now you look like the trash you are. And since you insist on trying to cover it up with makeup, your rich-bitch friends, and this, quite frankly, rude new attitude . . ." She shook her head like a disappointed mother scolding her child. I hoped to god Madison never had children. "Well, it's time to expose you. Completely. Lay you bare, so to speak, for the world to see. The football team has practice here tomorrow morning, right, Jayden?"

He nodded and gave her a bored "yeah."

She grinned. "Excellent. Then they'll see you. Maybe a few of them will even use you. That's all that lumpy body of yours is good for anyway."

I was getting a little confused. Were they just going to leave me out here all night? I could work with that. I could try to reach my phone as soon as they left.

Like an idiot, I let hope spark in my chest.

They crushed it almost immediately.

Madison reached into her jacket pocket and pulled out something small enough to fit in the palm of her hand. Slowly, she pulled the switchblade straight, giving the sharp edge of the knife a little stroke.

The others shared uncertain looks. Obviously, she

hadn't shared this part of the plan with them.

"Madison?" Bonnie was the only one brave enough to tentatively voice her discomfort.

But Madison ignored her. With every slow step she took toward me, the beating of my heart somehow ratcheted up even harder and faster. At this rate, I'd die of a heart attack.

I sobbed again and turned my head to the side.

She pressed the blade flat against the side of my nose, right at the edge of my birthmark.

"Maybe I should cut this out. It's so disgusting," she whispered close to my face as another sob shuddered through me. "But no, that would be doing you a favor. Don't wanna catch any diseases anyway."

Instead she trailed the knife down my cheek, over my jaw, and down my neck, moving to the middle of my chest.

She bunched the top of my T-shirt in her fist, adjusted her grip on the knife, and started hacking away at the fabric. She didn't stop until it was cut all the way down the middle, and then she pulled my bra away from my chest, wedged the knife between the cups, and cut that too.

The others stood by doing *nothing*, saying *nothing*, as Madison dragged the tip of the knife down my torso. Just before it reached my belly button, a flash of movement over her shoulder caught my attention.

Someone was running—sprinting across the field toward us. The sky was now nearly completely dark, only faint indigo light and the brightly shining moon making it possible to see.

He was halfway to us before I realized it was Turner. Relief warred with uncertainty in my chest.

Noticing my attention was on something behind them, the others all turned.

"Fuck," Madison muttered under her breath.

Bonnie looked as if she was ready to bolt, wide eyes flicking between Turner and me.

Madison's knife was still pressed to my belly.

Turner stopped just a few yards away, breathing hard, his shocked gaze taking the scene in.

Jayden recovered first and took a step toward him. "Hey, man. Let's get out of here and leave the girls to it."

Turner looked at him as though he'd only just realized he was there, then his eyes zeroed in on me—the cut-up clothing, my arms tied behind me, the mess that was my face.

I couldn't look away from his eyes, but I started to cry again.

I was out of my mind with fear, and in that moment, I had no idea what he might do.

Would he crack a joke, join them in torturing me?

Do nothing and just walk away, as he had every other time?

Snap out of his shock and try to help me?

Did I even *want* him to, knowing what it would mean for Jenny, for his family, for all that he'd sacrificed to get here?

Everything was so fucked up; I had no idea what the boy I loved would do next, and that almost broke me.

"What . . ." The single word fell from his lips softly, hanging in the moonlight between us. Then his eyes hardened, his nostrils flared, and he roared, "What the fuck is wrong with you people?"

Jayden dropped his friendly act and got in Turner's face. They were almost the same height. "Just walk away, Turner. This has nothing to do with you."

"Walk away and let you keep hurting her?" Turner pushed Jayden, who stumbled back. Without giving him a chance to recover, Turner threw his whole body behind a solid punch to the other boy's face. Jayden went down hard, clutching his nose.

Madison pointed the knife at Turner.

The other girls backed away, looking as though they wanted to run but were too afraid of what might happen if they did.

"Get away from him, you psycho!" I screamed as Madison swung the little switchblade. Turner leaned back, avoiding the swipe at his chest.

I pulled at my restraint in vain, the hard plastic digging farther into my wrists. My fingers were completely numb.

Turner lunged and grabbed Madison's wrist, stopping a second strike. With his other hand, he gripped a fistful of her hair and yanked. She cried out in pain, and Turner took the knife smoothly, tossing her to the ground as soon as he had it.

"Leave!" he bellowed. "Get the fuck away from her before I completely lose my shit!"

The girls backed away immediately, breaking into a

run when they realized he wasn't going to chase them down like the animals they were.

Madison helped Jayden to his feet. He looked as if he was considering having another go at Turner, but any idiot could see he didn't stand a chance, especially when Turner had the knife.

Madison sneered at me. "This isn't over."

Turner stepped between us, breaking her line of sight. "Oh, it's fucking over."

Without saying another word, they walked away. About halfway up the field, they started to bicker, gesturing with their hands, but by then, they were out of earshot.

Once he was sure they were gone, Turner rushed to my side, his hand hovering around my shoulder, beside my head, but not connecting. "Oh god, Mena." He sounded pained, his soul as tortured as my body.

I closed my eyes and cried some more. I hated that he was seeing me like this, even as a forceful wave of relief coursed through me. I hated that he was hurting. In that moment, I hated the whole fucking world.

Turner stepped behind me and carefully cut the cable tie. As soon as my arms were released, I collapsed to the ground, the wet grass squelching beneath my knees.

Despite my numb fingers, I managed to cover myself with the ragged bits of my T-shirt before slumping forward and completely giving in to emotion.

I was hysterical—crying, rocking back and forth, yelling as all the pain registered over and over in my overworked mind. My knees hurt where I'd fallen on them. My hands were in agony as the blood rushed back to my fingers. My shoulder ached from when they'd shoved me to the ground. My head pounded. My cheek stung.

My soul was the worst though—my soul was in tatters.

Turner wrapped his arms around me so gently—as if worried that if he pressed too hard, I might shatter. He was murmuring something, but his words didn't register. All I could focus on was the feel of his strong arms; his fresh, clean smell; the rocking motion of our bodies.

All that mattered was that he was there. He'd been there for me in the single darkest moment of my life.

I wrapped an arm around his waist, and he drew me closer into his chest, rubbing my back, kissing my hair.

"I'm here." His words finally broke through the fog of my shock, and I stopped sobbing. "You're OK. You're safe. I won't let them hurt you ever again."

"Shit." I gripped his jacket in one fist. "Turner, what about Jenny?"

"Shh. It's OK. Don't worry about that right now. We'll figure it out."

I had to take his word for it. I could cope with only so much at one time.

He stroked my hair. "I'm gonna call the police now, OK?"

"No." I pulled back to look into his eyes—his red, crying eyes. I held my T-shirt together with one hand

and stroked his cheek with the other, softening my voice. "Please, don't call the police."

He frowned. "OK, then let's find a way to contact a teacher or the principal to report them. There has to be some kind of after-hours emergency number."

I was shaking my head before he finished speaking. "No, Turner. They don't care. No one gives a shit what happens to me. Haven't you learned by now? I'm nothing. I don't matter."

No one cared about me. No one. How could this have happened to me if they did? What was the point in trying to tell someone when they didn't care to listen?

I wanted to get away from it all. I wanted to ignore the world as it had ignored me. I wanted my very existence to stop so this pain would stop too.

Turner looked angry. He huffed and shrugged out of his jacket, then draped it around my shoulder and helped me put my arms through the sleeves. "You're not nothing. You matter to me more than anything on this fucked-up world."

I stared at him. I didn't know what to say to that.

Moisture was seeping into my jeans. I shivered. "Just take me home, Turner. Please."

He gave me a searching look, then zipped up the jacket. "OK, Mena. Let's go home. I've got you."

He didn't let me even try to stand up myself. He just grabbed my broken phone, gathered me into his arms, and started to walk across the football field.

I rested my head on his shoulder and stared up at the impassive moon.

CHAPTER 17

I AWOKE WITH A START, BUT THE FEEL OF Turner's warm, comforting arms made me relax back into his side almost immediately.

"What . . ." I cleared my throat. It was sore from screaming for help, but that was the least of my worries. "What time is it?"

"Just after ten. You dozed off." He kept his ocean-deep voice low—a balm to my bruised soul.

I sighed against his shoulder and snuggled closer, staring out the window. His curtains were wide open, the moon intruding on our private moment.

The past few hours were a bit of a blur, but I'd obviously felt safe enough to fall asleep. Small victories. I remembered Turner shuffling me gently into the back of a cab, the driver grumbling about the short fare.

He hadn't let me walk when we were dropped off outside our building, scooping me right back into his arms. "Do you want me to come in with you? Talk to your parents together?" he'd asked.

"They're not home. I don't want to be alone. Take me to yours?"

He did as I asked, not even setting me down in the elevator. It seemed his dad was out too—his apartment was dark, silent. I hardly registered a couch, a kitchen as we passed.

I asked to use his shower, and he hesitated, fidgeting with the hem of his T-shirt. "OK, but . . ."

"What?"

"I know you don't want to go to the police or whatever, but can I take some photos first? Just so you have them. If you change your mind later." He eyed me warily.

I didn't want to think about why I might need them, what he wanted to take photos of. I just nodded.

The flash cut harshly through the darkness of his bedroom, and I closed my eyes. He took several photos— of my face, my wrists, my clothing. Then he shuffled me to the bathroom and got awkward again, asking if I needed help.

I'd managed without him.

I remembered thinking it felt good to be in his T-shirt and boxer briefs—comforting. We must have settled on the bed soon after.

The next thing I knew, I was starting awake.

"Are you hungry?" he asked.

I shook my head.

I wished we could stay like this forever, cocooned in the darkness, away from the rest of the world. But eventually, things started to creep back into my head—

ugly, insidious things crawling over my comfort and ruining everything.

I lifted onto my elbow to look at him. "Do you regret it?"

He frowned, so I clarified. "Saving me. Putting all your hard work to find your family at risk."

The frown disappeared, and his lips quirked into a barely there, sad smile. "No. Not even for a second."

"But what about your sister?"

He rubbed my feet with his. "They still don't know Jenny is my sister. We know where she is, and we won't let them disappear again. I'll talk to my dad in the morning, and we'll come up with a plan."

"Your dad is gonna hate me." I dragged a hand down my face.

Turner caught it and rubbed my knuckles gently. "No, he won't. He's going to love you. Just like I do."

I looked into his face, suddenly lost for words. Did he just . . .

He frowned slightly before rising up onto his elbows. Was he nervous? "Mena, I could never for a second regret standing up for you. I'm going to defend you with everything I have from now on. I'll walk you to every class if I have to. I'll beat Jayden's ass every time he looks at you. I'll report every little transgression against you to the school until they're sick of me. I'm going to do what I should've done from the start. Because you mean everything to me. The world is a shitty place, but you make me happy. I love you."

So much had happened that night. My body and my

soul were damaged, but my heart . . . Pure anguish had been writhing inside me; I'd thought I might never smile again. Yet there he was, pulling one out of me already.

"I love you, Turner." I closed the small distance between us and kissed him with a smile on my lips, this intoxicating feeling between us making me giddy.

It wasn't long before it turned to more. Our smiles fell away, and the kiss deepened, our tongues stroking.

He wrapped an arm around my waist, and I leaned forward, pushing him back against the pillows and pressing my chest flush with his. I swung a leg over his hips, and his other hand went to my knee. He trailed his fingers up my leg, then dipped them under the fabric of the boxer briefs to grip my ass.

I moaned and rolled my hips, seeking friction. He'd already given me *everything*, but I wanted more. My heart was full, but my body was greedy.

I moved until I was straddling him fully and ground myself against him. He was so hard that pressing too much was almost painful.

He gasped and broke the kiss, but I just kissed and licked down that sharp jaw to his neck, my hips never stopping, that heavy, heady feeling building low in my belly.

When my mouth reached the collar of his shirt, I frowned. There was too much fabric between us. I didn't want *anything* between us anymore. I wanted all of him, and I wanted to give all of myself right back.

I yanked him up into a sitting position and pulled his shirt off. He propped one hand behind himself for balance, his other gripping my hip. I stilled, and for a moment, we just drank in the sight of each other, breathing hard.

He was so beautiful, bathed in the silver moonlight streaming in through his window, all the dips and flat planes of his sculpted body accentuated. I ghosted my hands up his arms and leaned in, placing a soft kiss on his shoulder.

"You have freckles on your shoulders," I whispered against the adorable little spots, smiling. He had a few on his nose too, but they were faint, hardly noticeable unless you were nose-to-nose with him.

In place of a response, he dragged the tip of his nose up my neck and kissed the spot just under my ear. I shivered, but definitely not from cold. If anything, I was overheating.

I leaned back and whipped the borrowed T-shirt off.

Turner's eyes widened as he took me in, bare from the waist up and straddling his lap. It was clear where this was going. At least, I hoped it was clear. Did he not like my boobs? His stare had gone hard, fixed on something just below my chest.

I looked down. "Oh."

Madison must've nicked me with the knife after all. Compared with all the other injuries, the little cuts on my belly didn't really rate as something to worry about. I hadn't even registered them in the shower—although I had been in a bit of a haze.

Turner sighed and looked into my eyes. "Maybe we should slow down? Or just stop if you want to?"

"Do you want to?" I crossed my arms, covering my chest, and looked down.

He wrapped his arms around me and leaned back against the pillows. "No. I don't want to stop. Whatever you're thinking, put it out of your mind. You drive me crazy." To punctuate his point, he rolled his hips and ground his still very hard erection against me. I gasped, my body reminding me that it was still roaring to go.

"But, baby"—Turner ran a gentle hand through my hair—"I don't want to hurt you. After everything tonight . . . I just want to be careful."

I shook my head and lifted myself just enough to look into his eyes. "Don't. Turner, I don't want you to see me as some kind of broken, damaged thing. This is exactly why I didn't want you to know at the very start. I don't want this to define me."

"That's not how I see you, Mena. It's not about that. But it was only a couple of hours ago that . . ."

"Please." I didn't let him continue the thought. "I don't want to go there. I don't want to think about that right now. I want to be *here*, in this moment, with you. Make me feel good, Turner. Make me forget."

I let my voice go breathy at the end as I rubbed myself against him. His eyes grew hooded, even as I watched the indecision dance in their depths.

"Just to clarify . . ." he whispered, then moaned, his hips once again moving against mine.

"I want to have sex with you." I could feel myself blushing at the words, but I was proud I'd managed to get them out all the same.

"Fuck." The word tumbled out of his mouth on a heavy exhale, and he ran a hand through his messy hair. "Are you . . . is this your first time?"

"Yes." I bit my bottom lip. "Yours?"

He shook his head, and it took a conscious effort not to ask how many people he'd slept with. It didn't matter. In this moment, he was here, with me, and he loved me.

With gentle but deliberate movements, he rolled me onto my back and kissed me . . . and kissed me and kissed me until I could hardly breathe.

When he finally pulled his lips away, he rested his forehead against mine, our breath mingling. "It's probably going to hurt."

I chuckled. "I know. I'm not completely clueless."

He laughed lightly. "I wasn't suggesting you were. I'm just . . . I can't do anything to prevent that, but I want you to feel good first, so . . ."

He shifted onto his side, the length of his body pressed against mine, and propped himself up on one elbow. For a moment he simply stroked my cheek, then his gentle hand ran down my neck to circle each breast, caressing the undersides, trailing his fingers closer and closer to the nipples. I was breathing so hard my chest was heaving, every breath pushing my breasts farther into his touch.

Just when I thought I might die from this torture, he firmly kneaded first one, then the other, making me moan. I threaded my hands into his hair as he leaned down and took my nipple into his mouth, circling it with his tongue while his fingers played with the other.

Pleasure shot down to the spot between my legs, and I squirmed, rubbing my thighs together.

Turner responded by dragging his hot hand down my body. When he reached the waistband of the boxer briefs, I moved my hands down to help him remove them, taking a shuddering breath.

Holy shit. I was completely naked on a boy's bed. No—not just some boy. *Turner*—the boy I loved. This was really happening. I grinned at the dark ceiling, then reached for his underwear.

He lifted his head, another jolt of pleasure shooting down my spine at the sensation of cool air hitting my wet nipple. Gripping my hand gently, he guided it away from his crotch, and I frowned.

"I told you I wanted to make you feel good." He gave me a devious little smile and boldly stroked me between my legs.

I gasped, my knees instinctively widening as his fingers explored the most private part of my body.

It felt so good, but I didn't want to waste any more time. "I love you for wanting to do that, but I can't . . . uh . . . I won't be able to . . ."

He kissed my lips gently and whispered against them. "Come?"

My "yes" turned into a moan as he slowly slid one finger inside.

"You've never had an orgasm?" he asked, adding another finger.

I rolled my eyes. "I've had plenty of orgasms, Turner. On my own. But . . . no one else has been able to make me come before." Although I was questioning my doubt; the things he was doing with his fingers were making that delicious feeling build at the base of my spine. Until his hand stilled, that is.

He blinked once, then shook his head and smiled. "Sorry. My brain just short-circuited for a second. Thoughts of you making yourself come were warring with thoughts of beating the shit out of anyone else who's tried."

I laughed, then cried out in pleasure as his fingers started moving again, sliding in and out of me, creating the most incredible friction.

He dropped the smile and lowered his voice again. "Just tell me what you like, Mena."

I looked down at my naked body writhing under his touch, the erotic view of his hand between my legs, and decided to let him try. Taking a deep breath, I reached down for his hand and adjusted it until his thumb was over my clit.

"Rub here," I instructed, pushing down any awkward self-consciousness that was trying to make me feel weird about this.

"Like this?" He moved his thumb from side to side. It felt good, but it wasn't what worked for me.

"Up and down."

"OK." He changed direction immediately, and I began to roll my hips against his touch. "Does that feel good?"

"Yes," I breathed. "A little harder."

He increased the pressure and started moving the

fingers inside me again, finding a rhythm that had my whole body feeling as if it were about to combust.

"Fuck." A bit of surprise leaked into my tone. "Right there. Just like that. Don't stop."

I writhed against him and moaned, surges of pleasure shooting out from my core. My back arched as the intense orgasm washed over me. One hand gripped a fistful of Turner's hair, and the other tugged at the sheets, searching for something to hold on to so I wouldn't float completely away on this wave of intense pleasure.

Turner removed his fingers and stroked me gently as I came down, my hands releasing their death grip on hair and fabric.

"That was the hottest fucking thing I've ever seen." His voice was gravelly, strained.

Still panting, I leaned up to kiss him as I pushed his underwear down. This time he let me.

As our tongues battled for dominance, I wrapped my fingers around him and stroked. He groaned and pumped his hips into my hand.

A few short moments later, he broke the kiss and shifted out of my reach. "If we keep doing that, I'm gonna finish in your hand."

Without waiting for a response, he swung his legs over the side of the bed and reached into his bedside drawer. As he opened the foil packet and put the condom on, I lightly scratched his back, along the length of his spine. He hummed and rolled his shoulders, making the muscles in his back dance.

When he turned back to me, he captured my hand and placed a gentle kiss on my palm. "Do you want to be on top?"

I shook my head. "My legs are jelly."

"Are they?" He gave me a teasing smile as he positioned himself between them.

My witty retort died on my lips when I felt him, suddenly, *right there*. He leaned down to kiss me, pushing strands of hair off my sweaty forehead as he rubbed his length up and down.

Pulling back to look into my eyes, he reached between us, positioned himself at my entrance, and pushed in slowly, his eyes hooded, his teeth gritted. He got to what I guessed was halfway, then pulled back out, only to slide back in again.

I moaned lightly, gripping his shoulders. My body was still sensitive from my orgasm, everything warm and relaxed, and I was surprised to find I wanted more. Would I ever get enough of Turner Hall? My back arched and my hips rolled, seeking more, more, more. The stretching sensation was new but felt good.

Then he pushed farther in, and pain shot through my lower body. I winced and he stilled, kissed my cheek.

"Breathe, Mena. Try to relax."

My fingers were digging into his shoulders, my abdominals clenching against the intrusion. With a deep breath and a conscious effort, I relaxed my muscles and nodded.

He pulled out slowly, then pushed back in. There was pain again, but it wasn't as bad this time, and now he was all the way in, his hips flush with mine.

He smiled at me, and I smiled back before kissing him. He rolled his hips, grinding against me until I was panting and turning my head to the side in order to breathe.

With a groan, he started sliding in and out of me, gently at first, his chest grazing against my breasts with every stroke. Then his pace increased, his movements becoming more frenzied and uneven.

I reached one hand over my head, gripping the pillow, and dragged the other down his smooth back and all the way to his ass, fascinated by the way his muscles tightened and relaxed as he pumped his hips up and down, in and out.

It wasn't long before his whole body tensed and he released a long, low moan, burying his head in my neck as he came. Chest to chest, hearts beating frantically, we let our breathing even out for a few moments.

Turner kissed the side of my neck, then my cheek, then my nose, and finally my lips. "You OK?"

I smiled and kissed him again. "I'm perfect."

His returning smile was more than a little self-satisfied, and I couldn't blame him. As far as first times went, this one was pretty damn great.

He held the condom to the base of his penis as he pulled out. I wobbled to the bathroom and peed, relieved to see just a small amount of blood; cleaned up quickly; then returned to the dark room.

Turner was back on the bed, a fresh pair of boxer briefs on. He opened his arms, and I snuggled into his side. We held each other in silence, just breathing, just *being*, as I stared at the bright moon framed by the window.

That impassive, glowing sphere had witnessed my lowest moment and my highest peak all in one night.

The night was so still and silent that the sound of a phone vibrating cut through it like a bullhorn. I glanced over my shoulder, but Turner tightened his hold on me. "They can leave a message."

His voice sounded sleepy, gritty. I was ready to drift off at any moment too.

The phone buzzed again. We both sighed and waited for it to ring out.

Barely a few seconds later, it rang again.

With a growl, Turner reached for it, then frowned. "I don't know this number."

He showed me the screen. It didn't look familiar, so I shrugged.

With another dissatisfied smile, he answered it. "Hello?"

"Turner?" It wasn't on speaker, but the panicked voice of a young girl cut through the silent room all the same. "I need your help. I need you to come get me. I'm—"

Turner's whole body tensed, and he sat up. "Jenny? What's going on?"

He rushed to the other side of the room and turned on the light, the sudden brightness making me wince. I couldn't hear Jenny any longer as Turner rushed about the room, pulling his jeans up awkwardly.

Without anything else to change into, I pulled on one of his T-shirts and a pair of sweatpants from off the floor. The pants fit well around my hips, but I had to roll the legs up several times so I wouldn't trip over them.

"OK. I'm coming to get you." He was keeping his voice calm for her, but I could hear the tremble in it. Worry churned in my gut as I pulled my sneakers onto my bare feet.

"Jenny, take a deep breath and listen carefully." He stopped in the middle of the room, staring into space as he spoke quickly but clearly. "We're going to hang up in a minute. As soon as we do, you need to throw the phone away, OK? Throw it as hard and as far as you can. They can use it to find you. Then go and hide. Do not come out until I get there."

He listened for a few seconds. I thought I could hear a scared little voice crying.

"I'm already on my way. OK? Now *go*."

He hung up and turned his wide, panicked gaze to me.

CHAPTER 18

I HANDED HIM A T-SHIRT. "TURNER, WHAT'S going on? Is she OK?"

He pulled it over his head and shoved his feet in a pair of sneakers, tying them as he answered. "I don't know. She ran away from home. She's terrified." He stood and gripped my shoulders. "I'm so sorry, Mena, but I have to go get her. She's in Oak Hill Park. I'll have to sprint there."

"It's OK." I started to tell him to go get his little sister, then remembered Mom had picked Dad up on her way to my aunt and uncle's. "Wait! We can take my dad's car!"

"Yeah? OK. Let's go."

We were heading for the front door when the glint of the moon through the sliding door reminded me there was another way.

"Turner!" I yanked on his arm. "The balcony will be faster. Can you break the glass or something?"

"Good idea." He ran into the kitchen and came back

out with a butter knife, tucking it into his pocket.

Out on his balcony, he reached over the dividing railing to unhook and push aside the bamboo screen, the first and now the last remaining barrier between us. With ease and athleticism, he launched himself over to my balcony, knocking the rickety little chair over, then helped me clamber across. I didn't even have time to worry about how far the drop was before I was safely on the other side.

Turner yanked on the flimsy old sliding door, shoving it sideways as much as the latch would allow. Then he used the butter knife to flick the latch up, and we were inside my apartment.

I sprinted across the room and grabbed the car keys out of the little bowl as Turner wrenched the door open. After flicking the lock and slamming the door behind us, we tore down the corridor.

Waiting in the elevator to get down to the ground floor was torture. Turner tried to call his dad and cursed when he didn't answer.

We wedged out into the lobby before the elevator doors were even fully open. Heart hammering in my chest, I led the way to Dad's car and jumped into the driver's seat. I had to adjust it, my fingers fumbling on the bar under the seat as I cursed bloody murder.

I started the car and peeled out of the spot, the tires screeching as we took off.

"Which way, Turner?" I shouted. I knew the park he'd mentioned, but I'd been there only a handful of times and not recently.

He was already looking it up on his phone. "Turn right at the end." He pointed.

I glanced down at the clock in the dash, 10:56 illuminated in neon green.

For the next seven excruciating minutes, Turner directed me while trying to call and text his dad. I drove like a crazy person—flying past intersections, barely slowing down at stop signs, skidding around corners.

As soon as we reached our destination, I stopped the car with a lurch across three parking spots and killed the engine, and we both launched ourselves out of the vehicle, leaving the doors wide open.

"Jenny!" Turner bellowed as he ran across the grass. "Jenny! Where are you?"

"Turner!" Her high voice reached us before we could see her. Only seconds later, the young girl came running out of the pitch-black trees and into her brother's waiting arms.

I stopped halfway between them and the car, breathing a sigh of relief and resting my hands on my knees.

I couldn't make out what they were saying to each other, but Turner pushed her out and held her at arm's length, speaking earnestly while visually checking her for injuries.

I ran my hands through my hair, adjusted the sweatpants on my hips, and started walking over slowly.

". . . sure you're not hurt?" Turner's voice was somehow both stern and worried.

"Yes. Shut up. I need you to take me away. Can we go? Away from here. Just me and you," she pleaded, obviously panicked.

"What? What are you talking about? Jenny, what happened?"

She tugged his arm and tried to pull him in my direction, but he dragged her back to his side, still trying to calm her down.

Headlights appeared at the parking area's opposite entrance, snaking down the drive toward us. I frowned. Who would be out here this late?

"He killed Mom!" Jenny yelled. "He didn't know that I saw it, but Jayden knew, and then I couldn't take it anymore, and I ran away, and I think he knows now."

"Holy fuck. Who killed Mom? Where is she?"

"Boyd. It was about six months ago. Turner. She's gone." Jenny sobbed, and Turner hugged her, shooting me a desperate look.

But my focus was on the approaching car.

Dread washed over me like a waterfall as I realized why another car was in the park in the middle of the night. They were here for the same reason we were.

To get Jenny.

My suspicion was confirmed just as it articulated itself in my mind.

"Fuck. Turner?" I waved my hand to get his attention, my eyes still glued on the two men getting out of the car. They hadn't spotted us yet. "We have to go. Now."

"What?" He frowned, then looked over his shoulder.

Jenny followed our gazes and spotted them at the same time . . . and *screamed* as only a teenage girl could.

It pierced the night.

Turner and I took off at the same time, Turner dragging his little sister along with a firm grip on her wrist.

In the same instant, the two men looked over and started sprinting in our direction.

I kept glancing between the men and the waiting car—our only escape—as I pumped my legs. They were too close. They were going to cut us off.

Shit. Shit. Shit.

Turner realized it too. He pushed Jenny and me behind him, and I grabbed her skinny arm and pulled her close. She gripped my T-shirt as if her life depended on it, her whole body trembling in my arms.

As they got closer, Boyd threw an arm out to signal his son to stop running, then looked us over with his calculating gaze. Jayden's eyes widened as he glanced from me to Jenny to Turner and back again, trying to figure out how it all fit.

I suddenly felt sick.

I was face-to-face with one of my tormentors, mere hours after I was convinced he would kill me.

Every mean word, every shove, every sneer and look of disgust he'd ever thrown my way flashed through my mind. For a second my vision blurred, and I had to swallow down bile.

"Jenny, come here this *instant*." Boyd pointed harshly at the spot next to him, his voice the epitome of a chastising parent.

Jenny just plastered herself tighter against my side.

"She's not going anywhere with you." Turner's voice was deathly calm, but the tension in his body told me he was ready to explode at any second.

"Dude, what the fuck is with you tonight?" Jayden shook his head and narrowed his eyes in anger. "Give me my sister."

"*My* sister," Turner growled.

Boyd laughed lightly, the sound one of pure menace. "That's why you looked familiar. That bitch would not shut up about her other kid. The one she left behind. Kept wanting to go find you."

"What?" Jayden looked between them, genuinely confused. Did he not know? Unable or unwilling to process the situation, he stuck with anger. He took a step toward Turner and threw his arms out, looking as if he might throw a punch at any moment. "What the fuck is your problem?"

"*You*." Turner pointed at Jayden, then at his dad. "And him."

"You wanna go? Let's fuckin' go!" Jayden beat his chest with his fist, but I kept my focus on Boyd. He was staring at Jenny so intently it was making my skin crawl.

"I already put you on the ground once tonight," Turner responded, "and I've been itching to beat your sadistic ass to a pulp. Don't test me."

They were seconds away from throwing punches. Turner could easily take Jayden, but could he take both of them at the same time? Maybe Jenny and I could make a run for the car.

I glanced in its direction. The wide-open doors were barely a hundred feet away.

"That's enough!" Boyd roared. "Give her to me right now!"

Turner didn't reply. Instead he simply rolled his shoulders and lifted his hands, ready to fight.

My heart was beating so fast I thought I might pass out.

Jenny was crying hysterically.

With an angry yell, Jayden lunged. Turner dodged him, grabbing his shirt and using the momentum to shove him to the side. Jayden lost his balance and toppled, but in an instant, he was back on his feet.

The two boys clashed, throwing punches and kicks as Jenny and I inched backward. I was too scared to make an all-out run for it. What if Boyd grabbed us, hurt us? And what about Turner?

As if to prove my point, Boyd jumped into the fight. Between the two of them, they soon got Turner onto his back.

I looked between them and the car.

Stay and try to fight two men twice my size?

Or try to run and get help?

I had seconds, at best, before Boyd was no longer distracted with beating the crap out of my boyfriend. It was now or never.

I have to get Jenny to safety.

I have to help Turner.

Indecision churned inside me, tearing my heart down the middle. My eyes flew between the open car and a hefty branch, about the size of a baseball bat, on the ground next to us.

Run or fight? Fucking decide, Philomena!

CHAPTER 19

A BLUR OF MOVEMENT SPED PAST US, MAKING me gasp.

Turner's dad tackled Boyd and laid into him. "Keep your hands off my kids, you son of a bitch!"

After landing a few solid punches, he rushed over to where Turner had already thrown Jayden off, and helped his son to his feet. "You OK?"

Turner swayed and shook his head as if to clear it. "Yeah." He coughed, leaning over.

Jayden and Boyd were already limping away as fast as they could, throwing worried looks over their shoulders.

Turner's dad made to run after them. "Hey, get back—"

"Dad!" Turner stepped in front of him and placed a hand on his chest. "Let them go." He looked pointedly in our direction.

His dad's shoulders slumped, and he slowly turned to face us.

Turner walked to our side. I wrapped one arm around his waist while keeping the other around Jenny's shoulders, careful not to hurt him more.

"Jenny," their dad breathed, his daughter's name falling from his lips like an anguished prayer. He fell to his knees and stared at her as if she were some kind of miracle, his eyes filling with tears. "My baby girl. I missed you so much."

Jenny turned wide, watery eyes up to her brother, and he gave her a small, encouraging smile.

"I told you," he said, the deeper meaning lost on me.

Jenny looked at the grown man on his knees in a park in the middle of the night, then slowly made her way toward him. When she stopped only inches away, he didn't make a move to touch her. He kept very still, as if she were a rabbit that would bolt if he made the wrong move, said the wrong thing.

"Daddy." The word came out on a sob, so low I hardly heard it. Then she wrapped her skinny arms around his neck. He held her as if she might evaporate in his grip and gave us the biggest, most emotionally charged grin I'd ever seen on a grown man's face.

Turner and Jenny both refused to go to the hospital, and their dad didn't argue too hard for them to go—I had a feeling he was worried about what kind of questions might be asked. The man didn't want to lose his children.

Instead we went straight home. Turner's dad—who insisted I call him Simon and kept apologizing repeatedly that I got "dragged into all this crap"—

followed in his car behind us. Jenny wouldn't leave Turner's side, so they sat in the back as I drove at a much safer pace.

After we parked, Turner said he'd see me to my door. Jenny refused to go anywhere without him, and Simon declared he was never letting any of them out of his sight again. So even though I tried to protest, in the end all four of us piled into the elevator.

As the doors opened on my floor, several voices I recognized echoed down the hall. I winced and dragged my feet around the corner.

This was not going to be pretty.

Packed into the corridor in front of my apartment were my parents; Donna; her parents; my boss and Mom's friend, Leah; and two police officers. They were all talking over one another as the police officers tried to ask questions. My mom was crying, and so was my aunt.

Donna spotted me first.

"Mena!" She barreled past the others and ran straight to me, wrapping her arms so tightly around my neck I almost couldn't breathe.

"Hey," I croaked.

"I'm so glad you're OK," she whispered frantically. "I'm so sorry, but I was so fucking worried. I didn't know what else to do."

I pulled away and frowned. "What do you mean?"

"I told them." She managed to give me an apologetic wince before she was shuffled out of the way. Then it was my mom and dad cutting off my air supply.

"Guys," I wheezed. "Can't breathe."

"Oh my god." My mom held me out at arm's length. Her face was tear streaked, her hair a mess. "Is there something wrong with your lungs? Brad, we need to take her to the hospital."

"There's nothing wrong with my lungs. Would you calm down?" I bugged my eyes out.

"Calm down? *Calm down*?" She was doing the opposite of calming down. "Do you have any idea how worried we've been? When Leah called and told me you didn't show up for your shift . . . and then we came home and you weren't here, and the balcony door is busted . . . and then . . . when Donna told us . . ." She started crying again, covering her face with her hands for a moment. Then she took a deep breath and looked at me with some unfathomable emotion in her eyes.

Tears welled in my eyes too. I felt like shit for making everyone so upset—not that it was my fault. But it just rubbed salt in the wounds. The literal wounds I had on my body.

"Philomena." My dad's voice was low but barely restrained. "Whose clothes are you wearing?"

"Uh . . ." I glanced down at Turner's T-shirt and the sweats hanging off my hips. When I looked back up at my dad's face, he was staring daggers behind me—*at Turner*.

I stepped directly in front of my boyfriend, shielding him with my body, and threw my hands out. "None of this is Turner's fault. He saved me."

"Saved you?" Now my dad was confused.

I swallowed around a massive lump in my throat.

This was not how I wanted my parents to find out I was sexually active. In fact, I didn't want them to find out *at all*.

But that awkwardness was nothing compared to the anguish I felt at what I would have to do next.

"Yes. I got in some trouble tonight."

"Mena," Turner interjected, a hint of reproach in his voice as his hands landed on my shoulders. "You didn't just get in trouble. I think it's time you tell your parents the whole story."

Dad narrowed his eyes at the comforting hands on my shoulders.

I rolled my eyes. "Yes, I'm planning to. Can we just . . . go inside?"

We were all still packed uncomfortably in the dingy corridor. One of the fluorescent lights was flickering, and I really needed to sit down.

The radio on one of the police officers' shoulders crackled something unintelligible, reminding me they were there.

The other officer addressed us. "We have to attend an emergency situation, but we will need to speak to you all again. I'm glad your daughter is safe. We'll be in touch to take statements."

She smiled at my parents, and they rushed away.

Leah stepped up to kiss my cheek. "I'm glad you're OK."

"I'm sorry I missed my shift and didn't call. My phone is ruined."

"Don't worry about it." She gave me a reassuring

smile and turned to my parents. "I'm going to head home too."

"Thanks." Mom hugged her before Leah rushed off to catch the elevator.

"Want me to come in with you?" Turner asked.

What I wanted most was to collapse into bed and sleep for a week solid, but yes, I wanted him to hold my hand while I had the most difficult conversation of my life with my parents. I suspected he'd be more of a distraction though, judging by the dirty looks my dad was throwing him. Plus, he needed to be with his family. Jenny was leaning into her dad's side, asleep on her feet.

"No," I told him. "Go be with your family. Get some sleep. I think this is something I need to do alone."

"Are you sure?"

I turned to face him. "Positive. Go."

He pulled me in for a hug, and I melted into his warm embrace, drawing strength from his strong arms. He kissed the top of my head and released me, then walked away with his family.

I turned to face mine.

They all filed into the apartment, and I dragged my feet after them. Donna took my hand as I passed. "Not alone," she leaned in to whisper, picking up on what I'd just said to Turner. "Never alone."

I squeezed her hand and closed the door behind us.

CHAPTER 20

I DROPPED THE MASCARA IN THE MAKEUP CASE and smiled at my reflection in the mirror. I'd gone for an understated look with some subtle embellishment that made my dull blue-gray eyes pop. Turner kept saying how much he loved my eyes.

My hair was done too, sleek and straight, hanging down my back. I smoothed the front of my crisp white shirt with my hands, double-checking that I hadn't gotten any makeup on it.

It had been two weeks since that disaster of a night, and I hadn't been back to school or seen any of my classmates since. *Good riddance.* Today was my first day at Fulton Academy. My brand-new uniform fit me perfectly, the shirt sitting just right on my shoulders, the pleated skirt hugging my hips and stopping halfway down my thighs.

I frowned, wishing my thighs weren't so thick. But I pushed that thought away. I had enough shit to be nervous about without getting obsessed with how my thighs touched.

Of course, I knew the girls would be there with me, that I'd met all their other friends, that the staff had been informed of the situation at my previous school. But knowing didn't stop me from having intrusive, panic-inducing thoughts. What if the girls turned on me? What if I did something to piss them off and ended up friendless again? What if the other kids started picking on me? What if the teachers had just said what my parents wanted to hear and were actually just as apathetic as the ones at my old school? What if this was just a dream and I'd wake up any moment and have to go back to that hellhole?

I took a deep breath and leaned on the counter, staring at myself in the mirror. This was who I wanted to be—who I *was*. "You can do this Mena," I whispered to my reflection.

Part of me wanted to take the uniform off and just go back to bed, but it had been hard enough to get my parents to agree to this. No way was I going to jeopardize it.

That night, after Turner and his family left, I'd sat at the kitchen table and told mine everything.

When my mom got the voicemail that I hadn't shown up to work, Donna had suspected the worst. She'd told my parents I was being bullied and that she'd tried to help, but in the rush to get back and check our apartment, she hadn't had time to tell them the whole story.

That part fell to me. With my cousin by my side,

holding my hand, I told my parents how miserable my school life had been since we'd moved to Devilbend. When I got to some of the harder parts, my voice wavering, Donna jumped in and filled in blanks. I told them what had happened that night—everything minus the sex with Turner. I didn't think that part was relevant, and I certainly didn't want to talk about it with my parents and aunt and uncle.

There was a lot of hugging and crying, a lot of questions, but no plans were made. I collapsed into bed that night and stayed there the whole weekend.

Mom and Dad didn't even complain, bringing me food and coddling me between bouts of sleep. Turner came over a few times, and I heard Dad apologize for assuming the worst of him. He even thanked him for "taking care of his little girl," and I'm pretty sure they hugged—I heard that telltale thumping that indicated a man-hug in progress. Then he went and ruined it by threatening to break Turner's legs if he broke my heart.

It wasn't until Sunday afternoon that I started to come out of the cocoon of denial and think about what would happen next. Technically, I had school the next day, but as I dragged my butt into the shower, the only thing I knew for sure was that I was *not* going back there. I was done with that place and those people.

My aunt and uncle arrived with the girls while I was in the shower, and they all rushed in for hugs when I came out. Amaya held me the longest.

We avoided the elephant in the room and ate an

early dinner. It was nice to have them all there, hanging out, talking.

"Anyone want tea?" Dad headed into the kitchen to boil the water as Harlow and Donna cleared the table.

I couldn't hold it in any longer. "I don't want to go to school."

Everyone paused. Mom patted my hand gently. "You don't have to. Take a few more days off. We still need to get you to a doctor. And the police have called twice about taking a statement. Your father and I will go there tomorrow." Her eyes had gone hard, her lips in a thin line.

Dad leaned on the counter as the water started to percolate behind him. "They're not going to get away with this, Philly. Not anymore."

"Once we've sorted everything out, then you can go back." Mom gave me a smile.

I frowned and shook my head. "No. I don't want to go back at all. And I don't want to talk to the police or the school. I just . . . I'm done thinking about this and worrying about it and having it consume so much of my energy. I just want to put it behind me."

Mom's gaze filled with pity. "Sweetheart, you have to go to school. It'll be fine once we speak with the principal. I'm going to demand that those kids are expelled. We're going to press charges."

She was making decisions for me, not listening to what I wanted. I'd spent my whole life trying not to be a bother to my family, trying to grit my teeth and bear it. But something had broken inside me that night—and something had broken *out*. Maybe it was a backbone. I pulled my hand out from under hers and shook my head again. "No. I am not stepping foot in that school again. I'm done."

"Philomena," Dad jumped in. "You can't just not go to school, and there's nowhere else that's close enough."

My aunt cleared her throat and shifted in her seat. "She could go to Fulton Academy."

"It's an excellent school. We could make some calls on your behalf tomorrow," my uncle quickly added. A little *too* quickly, making me wonder if they'd discussed this already.

Donna and Harlow stopped in the middle of making tea for everyone, the looks on their faces hopeful. Amaya gripped my knee under the table. I could practically feel the excitement radiating off her.

But I couldn't let it spread to me because . . .

"Emily, you know we can't afford that," my mom gritted out.

"We'll cover everything." Aunt Emily's eyes were pleading as she leaned forward on the table. "Fees, uniform, books, excursions, anything else she needs. It's your money anyway, Eleanor."

"No, it's not." Mom folded her arms. "Our mother disowned me for marrying the man I love and then left all her money to you. I don't want a single cent of it."

"Well, she's dead now and it's my money, and I want to give it to *you*." Emily threw her hands up.

I sighed, sharing a look with Donna and Harlow. Our moms had this argument often.

"I don't want it. Why are you doing this?"

"Because I love my niece!" my aunt yelled, clearly frustrated. "Because I want to do all I can for her. Because I love *you*, you idiot, and I want to help. Why are you letting pride get in the way—"

"Screw you. This is not about pride." Mom got up and leaned on the table. If previous fights were anything to go by, this was headed downhill fast; one of them would be storming out soon, both of them in tears.

Frustration bubbled up inside me. I brought both my hands down on the table with a bang, making everyone turn to me in shock.

"Shut up!" I yelled. "God, aren't you sick of having the same fucking argument already?"

"Language." Dad pointed a reproachful finger at me from the kitchen.

Ignoring him, I stood up and pulled my shoulders back. "Aunt Emily, Uncle Richard, thank you, I'd love to go to Fulton. Mom, Dad, either it's this or I don't go."

My mom turned her anger on me. "You are not dropping out of school."

"Would you rather I keep coming home with bruises?" I yelled into her face, holding my raw wrists up. "Would you rather I don't come home at all one day?"

She reeled back, eyes wide, but I was on a roll. "I'm not going back there. You can't force me. I'll be eighteen in a few months anyway. I'll get a job and move out if I have to."

"Of course I don't want you to get hurt." Mom

sounded tired now. "But things will be better once we talk to the school and the police. Maybe we can move . . ."

She looked to Dad, who was leaning on the counter, his head hanging between his shoulders. He sighed, then walked over to wrap his arm around her. My heart constricted in my chest. He was going to side with her—this was their "united front" position.

"Philomena will be going to Fulton," he said, surprising us all. "Thank you so much, Emily and Richard. We really appreciate your help."

"Brad." Mom tried to shrug him off, but he held on.

"It's what's best for her, Eleanor. You need to let this past resentment go. *Look* at her."

They both looked at me. I fidgeted with my sleeves but didn't back down, meeting their gazes head on.

My mom's shoulders slumped, and she nodded.

Donna, Harlow, and Amaya all screamed in excitement and enveloped me in hugs. I hoped seeing how loved and supported I was by them would help Mom see that this was the right decision.

"The police are still going to want a statement about why you went missing, honey," Dad said. "That's going to make it hard to avoid the full story."

In the end, I conceded to reporting the whole awful thing to the police and agreed to let my parents go down to the school and raise hell—as long as I didn't have to go.

With Turner backing up my story and with the evidence online, the police were able to press charges, and the school board expelled the students involved. Kelsey caved in to pressure (that I was pretty sure came from Donna) and turned on her friends, taking a slap on the wrist in exchange for her statement.

It took a couple weeks to sort out my late enrollment at Fulton and get my uniform and supplies, but my first day had finally arrived.

With one last deep breath and a final check of my hair and makeup, I grabbed my blazer and brand-new backpack off the bed. The backpack was a new school gift from my aunt and cost more than I made at the diner in six months.

"Oh my . . ." Mom covered her mouth with her hand, then dropped it to give me a watery smile. "You look beautiful, Philly."

"You kind of look like your mom when we first met. The uniform hasn't changed much. You look lovely, Sweet Chilly," Dad added. They'd both taken the morning off to be there for me on my first day. I'd drawn the line when they'd tried to insist on driving me themselves.

"Thanks, guys." I smiled and pulled on my shoes.

My new phone—a top-of-the-line new school gift from Donna and Harlow—vibrated in my pocket.

"I gotta go. The girls are here." I slung my expensive bag over my shoulder as giddy excitement mingled with nervousness in my gut.

"You haven't even had breakfast," Dad chastised.

"I'm too nervous to eat." I waved him off. He huffed, but they let me leave after kisses and lingering hugs.

The girls were waiting for me at the curb, all three leaning on Donna's car and looking stunning in their perfect uniforms. Amaya's skirt was the shortest, although it might have just been her ridiculously long, smooth legs making it seem like that. Donna looked as if she owned this town and everyone in it, big dark sunglasses framed by her short, sharp blonde hair. Harlow had her hair in two messy buns, her massive white headphones hanging around her neck. She was the first one to spot me.

She grinned and cupped her hands around her mouth. "Woohoo! You look hot!"

I laughed and looked away, embarrassed but also flattered. Donna and Amaya joined in, and they all started catcalling me worse than a construction site full of unsupervised apprentices.

"Work it!" Donna pumped her fist in the air.

"Shake that ass!" Amaya turned sideways and started shaking her own, the movement of the pleated skirt making the action even more obscene.

Fighting giggles, I gave in and played along, dancing on the spot and flicking my hair.

A loud wolf whistle sounded from behind me, and a deep male voice joined in. "Work that tight body, baby!"

I startled, my heart flying into my throat before I realized it was Turner.

The girls all cracked up laughing. I flipped them off, then turned to give my boyfriend a smack on the shoulder. He chuckled and gripped my hips, flashing me that mesmerizing smile of his.

"You scared me," I scolded but melted into him, wrapping my hands around the back of his neck.

"I'm sorry." He leaned down and nuzzled my nose. A chorus of "awws" came from the peanut gallery, and I rolled my eyes, trying to ignore them. Turner lowered his voice. "Wanna come over to my place after school? And leave that uniform on. I've always wanted to defile a private school girl."

"Dammit, Turner, now I'm gonna be distracted all day."

"Excellent." He grinned and closed the tiny distance between us, giving me a firm, languorous kiss. His tongue swiped my bottom lip, and I opened my mouth to him on a sigh, completely forgetting we had an audience. One of his arms circled my waist, drawing me tightly against him, as his other hand went to my neck, his thumb tracing my jaw.

My eyes flew open, and I broke the kiss, pulling his hand away from my face. "You'll ruin my makeup."

"You don't need it."

I frowned. Today was my first day of being who I really wanted to be; maybe I needed to make a statement about this. "I don't wear it just to look pretty for you, Turner, or anyone else. And I don't wear it to hide my birthmark. I wear it because I *like it*, I enjoy putting it on, and it makes me feel confident."

He blinked once, surprised at my outburst, then smiled. "I know. I didn't mean it like that. You look beautiful with the makeup on, baby. But you look beautiful without it too. *You* are beautiful, and I love you."

I melted at his words. "I love you too," I told him before going in for another kiss.

An exaggerated gagging sound from the direction of the apartment building had us pulling apart again.

Jenny was sticking her finger in her open mouth, making the universal sign for disgust. "You guys are so gross."

This time, we laughed along with the girls.

"Don't you worry, Jenny baby," Amaya called. "There will come a day, very soon, when you think kissing boys is the exact opposite of gross."

"Or girls!" Harlow chimed in. "Whatever you're into."

Turner gave them a murderous look. "No, she won't. Shut up!"

It was adorable how protective he was of his little sister.

In the days after everything exploded, Turner had needed to have some difficult conversations with his family too.

Simon was shocked and deeply saddened when he found out his wife was dead. He'd wanted Turner and Jenny to have their mother *and* their father in their lives. On top of his own grief, it crushed him to accept they would never have that again.

Turner was absolutely devastated. He'd spent years missing his mom, fantasizing about seeing her again, working to make that happen—and now he had to mourn her absence in his life for good.

Two nights ago we'd been sitting on his balcony together when the electricity had gone out again. In the silent darkness, he told me the worst thing about it was that he never got a chance to say goodbye. His shaky inhale right after made me tear up too. We held each other long after the electricity hummed back on.

Short of taking Jenny and going on the run for the rest of his life, there was no way for Simon to avoid speaking with the police to clear everything up. Due to the fact that Jenny was Simon's actual daughter and adamantly wanted to stay with him, CPS allowed them to remain together. Jenny also told the police how she'd seen Boyd throw her mom down the stairs, that it wasn't a tragic accident, as he'd reported at the time. Boyd had been taken into custody and was awaiting charges. Jayden was too, for the part he'd played in hurting me, but he had no other family here, and it looked as if he'd be sent off to live with an uncle in Wisconsin when everything was settled.

BestLyf had been very quick to release a statement severing all ties with Boyd Burrows and condemning his actions. They weren't being very cooperative with police though, and apparently it was proving difficult to get warrants to search Boyd's office at work.

Simon and Turner were disappointed that BestLyf's involvement in their wife and mother's tragic situation— all the manipulation and deceit—would likely never be proven, but they were at least satisfied her murderer would be brought to justice. I didn't really know what to think of their adamant belief that BestLyf was a cult. Had his mom really been brainwashed? Or had she found herself in an abusive relationship with a controlling, manipulative man who just happened to work for them? Perhaps it was a combination of the two. I didn't see the point in dwelling on it—Simon and Turner were just happy it was all over.

They were ecstatic to have Jenny back, and they both doted on her. At first, Simon had considered taking his kids and leaving, getting far away from this place. Turner and I could hardly even talk about what that would mean for us, but thankfully, Simon quickly abandoned the idea.

Jenny was at the start of a long road to unlearning all the negative things that had been put in her head about her father, to healing from all that she'd seen and experienced. But her new therapist had suggested moving could be detrimental. She had friends here, familiar surroundings, teachers she liked. Plus, her mom was buried in the Devilbend Memorial Park, and they wanted to be able to visit her. So they stayed.

I'd nearly choked up with relief when Turner told me. The thought of losing him was unbearable.

I was in therapy too. We all were. So. Much. Therapy.

"Good morning, Jenny." I extracted myself from Turner's arms and smiled at his little sister. She beamed back and gave me a tight hug. We'd formed a deep bond oddly fast—shared trauma tended to do that to people.

"You look really nice in your uniform, Mena," she told me.

"Thanks. You look beautiful too."

"Thanks! Turner, let's go. I don't wanna be late." She tugged on his arm, and he rolled his eyes at me, but there was no missing the affection there.

It was their first day back at school too. Part of me wished I could be with them, walk there together, spend my days with him. But I knew going to Fulton was the right move—it was the best move for me.

"Have a good first day, baby." Turner gave me one last peck on the lips before letting his kid sister drag him down the street.

"I will. Bye, guys!" I waved after them, then walked to my friends.

They each gave me a hug and put their sunglasses on. It was a ridiculously bright morning—not a cloud in the sky. Harlow pushed a caramel-flavored cup of diabetes into my hands as we piled into Donna's car.

"And I know you haven't eaten." Amaya thrust a small paper bag at me from the back seat. I took it and peeked inside.

"The best croissants in Devilbend," Donna informed me as she pulled into traffic.

"I'll be the judge of that." I took a massive bite, then paused to moan around the soft, flaky, buttery goodness. "Fuck. This *is* the best croissant in Devilbend. Maybe all of California."

"Told you," Donna sang from the driver's seat.

"Hurry up and finish it." Amaya smacked my

shoulder.

"No," I mumbled around another bite. "I wanna savor it."

"Ugh! Here!" Harlow leaned forward and yanked the drink and paper bag out of my hand. I just barely managed to snatch the rest of the croissant back and stuff it into my mouth with a glare. She just grinned back.

I chewed, and when my mouth was free enough to form words, I turned to face the back seat. "What the fuck—"

"Here!" Amaya thrust a rectangular box with a big bow on it at me. I took it reflexively and frowned. "It's your new school gift. I know the others already gave you theirs."

I sighed and smiled at them all. "You guys don't have to keep buying me shit. I'm happy just being able to hang out with you every day."

"We know," they chorused.

"Open it." Harlow waved her hand at me.

I let excitement win against the uncertainty. They were just being generous and loving on me—this was not about pity for the poor girl.

I ripped the paper off and opened the box.

Inside was a pair of sunglasses with a label I'd never dreamed I could afford. They were dark, like all of theirs, but had a slight point at the corners, reminding me of winged eyeliner. I tried them on and looked in the mirror.

"They're perfect. I love them. Thank you so much,"

I said and meant every word.

Amaya squeezed my shoulder.

We pulled into the parking area not long after. Before we could start walking toward the building, Donna dropped her bag and pulled out her phone. "We need to commemorate this moment."

We leaned on the hood of her car and squished in, smiling and pulling faces as she took several selfies.

She posted one immediately, and my phone buzzed in my pocket with the notification. She'd chosen one where we were all hugging, smiling widely, the sun glinting off our sunglasses. The caption was just one hashtag—#DevilbendDynasty.

I knew in that moment I'd always been a part of them as far as they were concerned. I was finally embracing it.

Donna and Amaya led the way, and Harlow and I hooked arms as we followed. I held my head high and waved to people I knew. I had a feeling it was going to be a good day.

NOTE FROM THE AUTHOR

Thank you so much for reading Like You Care! I really hope you enjoyed it and you'll consider leaving a review. And if you didn't like it, that's OK too – I'm always open to feedback.

ACKNOWLEDGEMENTS

First and foremost, thank you to John – my real-life romance novel, my constant support, my epic love. I couldn't do any of this without you by my side.

As always, thank you to my friends and family for your support and encouragement in all I do.

Thank you to Samantha Dove, Christine Estevez from Wildfire, Kirstin Andrews, my writers' group and my beta readers. Each and every one of you helps me to shape, polish, improve and ultimately, put out the best version of my book possible. I am beyond grateful!

To everyone involved in the Bully Me anthology (where Like You Care first appeared) thank you for giving me the opportunity to be a part of it. I learned so much. But thank you especially to CoraLee June who encouraged me to dip my toe into this dark side of romance in the first place. You believed I could do it and that means so much!

To all my readers – whether you've been with me from the start and comment on every single post in my reader group; or whether you've only just read Like You Care and never heard of me before – I would be nothing without you. I write for me, because it feeds my soul and I don't know how to stop – but I publish for YOU. Every email, message, comment, and messenger pigeon makes my day. Knowing that people are reading my words is such a humbling feeling. I'll never tire of it!

ABOUT THE AUTHOR

Kaydence Snow has lived all over the world but ended up settled in Melbourne, Australia. She lives near the beach with her husband and a beagle that has about as much attitude as her human.

She draws inspiration from her own overthinking, sometimes frightening imagination, and everything that makes life interesting – complicated relationships, unexpected twists, new experiences and good food and coffee. Life is not worth living without good food and coffee!

She believes sarcasm is the highest form of wit and has the vocabulary of a highly educated, well-read sailor. When she's not writing, thinking about writing, planning when she can write next, or reading other people's writing, she loves to travel and learn new things.

To keep up to date with Kaydence's latest news and releases sign up to her newsletter here:

kaydencesnow.com

Join her reader group here:
facebook.com/groups/KaydenceSnowLodge

Or follow her on:

Facebook: facebook.com/KaydenceSnowAuthor
Instagram: instagram.com/kaydencesnowauthor/
Twitter: twitter.com/Kaydence_Snow
Goodreads:
goodreads.com/author/show/18388923.Kaydence_Sn
ow
Amazon: amazon.com/author/kaydencesnow
BookBub: bookbub.com/profile/kaydence-snow

ALSO BY

KAYDENCE SNOW

Variant Lost: The Evelyn Maynard Trilogy - Part One
Vital Found: The Evelyn Maynard Trilogy - Part Two
Vivid Avowed: The Evelyn Maynard Trilogy - Part
Three
Just Be Her
It Started With A Sleigh

Printed in Great Britain
by Amazon